The Spitfire Series

The Mouth

Lady Boss

Beautiful Assassin

By Jordan Silver

Table of Contents

Prologue

"Patrick I need a solid old friend."

"Roberto is that you? how the hell are you my friend it's been ages? I hear you're having a little headache out your way is that what this is about? You need I should get some of my people on it?"

"Nah paisan, I've got it covered it's my baby girl; you remember Arianna yes?"

"Little Arianna is she still such a spitfire?"

"Mama mia if the enemy's bullet doesn't cut me down that child will do it I swear."

"A handful huh."

"And then some, that's why I'm calling; I need to send her to you for safe keeping until I send my enemies to hell where they belong. This fucking gumbah Vasili is a pain in the ass, now he's not only greedy but stupid. Word is him and his brother has concocted some scheme to force my little angel into marriage with one of their sons."

"Unethical, who would do such a thing to a young girl, what is she seventeen, eighteen?"

"She just turned eighteen but that's not the problem so much; the thing is she somehow got wind of it and is out for blood."

"Come again."

"The girl fancies herself to be some sort of gangster, my fucking idiot brother's always filling her head with shit. Instead of baby dolls and tiaras he had her playing with epees and shuriken. By the time I figured out what the fuck it was too late. While I was busy building an empire that fuck was turning my kid into his nephew.

"You know Alphonso was always set in his own ways and since he never planned on marriage and kids I guess he figured yours were gonna be his.

Patrick laughed at his old friend's plight; though the two men hadn't seen each other in quite some time; years in fact, he remembered well their younger days together. Days spent on the streets of Chicago as young toughs trying to make names for themselves. The old regime had been on its way out then and they were determined to make their mark. There'd been a war back then too, the old war horses hadn't wanted to let go but the young blood proved to be too much and youth and brains prevailed. The mob took on new connotations then; yes they still strong armed those who would oppose them but they were no longer in the market for unprecedented killings. Blood on your hands was seen as a last resort whereas before it had been par for the course. Back then in the back alleys of a festering city two young toughs had made a pledge in blood.

"Do you remember our oath? "Patrick now asked Roberto.

"I thought you'd forgotten it's been so long."

"Nah circumstances calls for a little change in plans but it's still the same; besides it works out better this way since my Paddy is more into the saving of lives. He has no stomach for the life; now his firstborn Shane, perfecto."

"Yeah? We'll have to sit down; I think that might be just what the doctor ordered."

"That much trouble is she?"

"If she wasn't my kid I would've capped her a long time ago does that answer?"

"Send her to me, I'll straighten her out."

Little did he know while he made that pledge to his old friend that things would change almost overnight.

Chapter 1

My name is Shane Flanagan those who know me and even some who don't fear me. In my line of work this is a good thing, a very good thing.

You see I'm a very bad man, bad to the motherfucking bone. I make no excuses for myself. I would stomp a motherfucker just for fun, well maybe not so much these days, but when I was younger, yeah.

Now I would shoot a motherfucker for stepping on my kicks and it didn't matter if they were Chucks or Gucci. It all depended on what kind of mood I was in, and who's doing the mother fucking stepping.

But I digress, as I was saying people feared me all over this fucking place, so tell me then why this little slip of a girl thought she could mouth off at me and get away with it?

Now this Arianna Rossi is a real pain in the ass, know what I mean?

She lived upstairs of this pub that I'd just requisitioned from its previous owner. I needed her place for something else so she had to go.

It's not like I was throwing her out in the street or some fuck. I owned enough residential buildings, all of them way nicer than this piece of shit that I could hook her up with a new pad, but no. She had to dig in her heels giving me shit about tenant's rights and lease laws and fuck all. The fuck?

She must not have heard.

Anyway my little stepbrother James went to see Miss. Rossi on my behalf for the one hundredth time and apparently this crazy ass chick had hauled off and shot him in the ass.

Now James is a lying fuck, so I took his version of events with a grain of salt.

That's why I'm here now in my office at my new pub, sitting across from the pain in the ass, who didn't seem to know I could end her in ten seconds.

"So Miss. Rossi, we meet again."

Crazy lady rolled her eyes at me. I looked over to my right hand man Michael who seemed to be having trouble not laughing.

Of course he would find this shit funny, his wife, my sister Sophia wasn't much better in the crazy stacks. In fact all the bitches around here seemed to either be on the rag or plum mother-fucking nuts. Except my ma, ma was an angel among women.

Now as for James, that fuck wasn't really my stepbrother, he's not my father's son and he's not my mother's, rumor had it that my grandfather who I inherited the business from used to mess with his mother.

How the fuck he ended up in my house is a mystery, but I was a kid when all this shit happened so I don't know fuck.

Grandpa stepped down three years ago when I turned twenty three.

Dad's a heart surgeon, he's as far removed from this shit as you can get. I take lives, he saves them. We have running debates on the subject every Sunday at the dinner table, but that's for another time.

Right now I'm trying to figure out what to do with 'the mouth'.

"Why did you shoot my little brother?"

"I should've known he was another pig."

Michael almost choked the fuck.

"Do you know who I am Miss. Rossi?"

"Yeah yeah, the big bad Shaney Flanagan, so what?"

Did she just call me Shaney?

I had to glare at Michael to shut him the fuck up.

"So you're not afraid of me huh?"

"Contrary to what has been written, I don't believe in playing poor and helpless to give my enemy a fake sense of power before he attacks, I believe in kicking them in the balls to start shit off."

"You read Sun Tzu?"

"What's it to you?"

"Just wondering why a little girl like you would be reading the Art of war."

"Because I have to deal with dumb motherfuckers every day, next question."

This chick was fucked in the head, there's no other explanation. I can't off someone who's touched, ma would have my hide.

Besides I could think of better uses for that mouth of hers.

Chapter 2

Well you've gone and cooked your goose but good haven't you Ari, are you insane?

I'm sitting here wondering why the hell my mouth won't stay shut, now mind you I give as good as I get, but this is Shane FUCKING Flanagan, the guy takes out people for less and here I am giving him shit.

I blame my dad, my dad rest his soul, always taught me, 'never show fear' if you can't fight your way out of it, talk your way out.

Well looks like your sage advice was about to get me whacked daddy. It wasn't just that either, for some reason I wanted to show this, specimen, that he was just a man, if I nut kicked him I'm sure I'll get the same reaction as I'd get from Joe the bum up the street.

Now he's studying me like an insect under a microscope, study away buddy, when you figure it out let me in on it, hell if I know what my problem is.

"Well, did you have anything else to ask me, some of us actually work for a living?" See, my mouth had finally had enough of me and decided to get me done in, or maimed one or the other.

"You still haven't told me why you shot him."

"Oh that, I didn't like the cut of his pants, people shouldn't wear their butt crack for the world to see, first of all it's tacky as all hell and secondly it's unsanitary , why the CDC haven't cried outbreak on that shit yet is beyond me." That's right Ari dig your grave just that much deeper by being a smart ass.

"Are you on some kind of medication for this shit lady?"

"What shit, you think I'm crazy cause I'm not afraid of you Capone?" He put his head in his hand and started muttering under his breath, I think he was saying the Latin mass, sounded like something I'd heard in church eons ago.

"Babe, seriously answer the fucking question so we can both get on with our lives."

"What difference does it make, you’re not going to believe me over your precious brother anyway, and I hate wasting my breath, you never know when you'll end up in an enclosed room with no air, and you'll wish you'd saved that wasted breath."

Okay I heard that loud and clear this time; he'd muttered an insult under his breath but not far enough under. He's been doing that the whole time.

"Well if you wish I'd save my breath this time stop asking me questions." I was on a roll, I think. The big guy in the corner was red faced and he kept puffing out his cheeks, I think he might be constipated, poor thing.

"Arianna, answer, the fucking, question."

Okay, he didn't yell but let me tell you, those words, said in that particular tone, in that particular way meant business. I'm not stupid, I wanna live, I've got shit I wanna do.

"He put his hands ...somewhere he shouldn't."

I saw him straighten up in his chair on full alert. What the hell?

"What did you say?"

Oh, yeah, I had kinda whispered that but I'm sure he heard me. I repeated it louder anyway and watched as his face reddened. I hope that anger wasn't at me. Stupid, why didn't you grab your gun on the way out the door? Because I didn't have time that's why.

"Tell me."

And I knew this was not the time to be snarky, he was pissed the fuck off, I don't know why though, the guy killed people for a living why should he care if his brother grabbed my ass?

"Not much to tell, he grabbed my ass, I gave him the impression I was interested and wanted to go put on something sexy just so I could get to my gun in the other room, at which time he saw said gun and tried to run, that's why he got it in the ass and not the balls."

"You were going to shoot him in the nuts for touching your ass?"

"My ass, my territory, I call the shots."

He looked over his shoulder kinda.

"Get his ass in here."

"Well, if you're having a family reunion I need to be going I've got shit to do."

"Sit down Rossi."

"Look buddy, you might have all day to sit around and pal around, but I've got to make a living. And since you've closed down this pub where I made that living, I need to hit the pavement to find a job. Capisce? "

"I'm not Italian."

I rolled my eyes at that; I've heard that word in every mafia movie known to man.

"Maybe we can work out the same kind of arrangement you had with the old man."

"What kind of arrangement?"

"I don't know, what kind of arrangement did you have, I mean your rent is a joke, no way that's the going rate in this neighborhood even if it is a piece a shit. So you must've been paying it off some other way, plus he gave you a job right downstairs, pretty cushy if you ask me."

"Are you implying, ...did you just, ... where's my gun? Hey you, in the corner, let me see your gun for a minute?"

"Ahhhh." that was his bright answer.

"Would you settle down?"

"No I will not settle down, I'm eighteen years old; Paulie has to be a hundred and ten and you're implying that I slept with him for a job and a subpar apartment? How dare you?"

"Calm the fuck down Rossi before I make you, and the next time you threaten me you better be ready to back that shit the fuck up, don't think for a second that I won't do a woman."

I was mad as hell but I was also unarmed and defenseless, not that I would really draw down on him, I'm not entirely stupid, but damn he made me mad with that crack.

"I'm not apologizing to you so stop sulking."

Oh will the insults never cease? I gave him a good glare for that one.

"Go fuck yourself." Oy, where the hell did that come from? Thankfully it just seemed to stun him, not send him into a homicidal rage.

"What am I gonna do with you?"

"Let me go find a job."

"Is waitressing your only qualification?"

"I'm in school, waitressing is flexible and it pays well." I shrugged my shoulders.

"How about I give you a job in one of my clubs or restaurants whatever you choose, I'm sure you'll be making a hell of a lot more than you were here."

"What's the catch?"

"I need you to move out of here in a week, I'll hook you up with a nicer place for the same shit money you're paying here. Do we have a deal?"

"Two things, first I have to see the apartment and the club, and second as long as you remember my last name is Rossi and not Magdalene."

"What the fuck?"

"I think that's the lady in the bible..."

"I know who it is Mikey."

"Well, now that we've got that covered when can I see this place?"

"Just like that, after two weeks of your bullshit?"

"You didn't ask before, you ordered."

"Ord...Are you fucking shitting me?"

"I shit you not."

Chapter 3

What the hell am I gonna do with this girl, she was driving me batty and that was saying a lot.

With two sisters who cornered the market on bitchy, I have my fair share of experience dealing with this shit, but 'mouth ' took the fucking cake.

I've never met anyone like her, neither man nor woman. If she'd been a dude I would've capped her ass already, just for the aggravation alone.

She was one cool customer too this one. I know she was afraid, not scared shitless, but she wasn't stupid enough not to appreciate the danger, not to fear me, but she held up well. No one would ever suspect to hear that mouth of hers.

When my second lieutenant and brother in law Anthony showed up with a hobbling James I was ready to be done with this shit.

Not with her, but with the situation.

Her I think I will be dealing with for a long time to come.

"You!" the dumb fuck started off on the wrong foot already. Pointing at 'mouth' with a scowl while hopping on his crutches.

"Hey Jimmy, how's your ass?" she made a pistol out of her fingers and shot at him.

Lord why me, the Staccos couldn't take me down so you sent this nut job to finish me off? She had to be somebody's idea of a secret weapon.

"Why you little bitch." he made as if to go after her. I didn't like that one fucking bit; if anyone was gonna go upside 'mouth's' head it will be me.

"James settle the fuck down. Now you wanna tell me again what the fuck happened up there?"

"Hey man I already told you." He was starting to sweat already.

"Tell me again." I know this guy's a fuck up of the first order but he knew better than to fuck with me. If I didn't like what he had to say, I just might put my foot in his ass.

"Start talking."

"Like I said, I knocked on the door and told her who I was and why I was there. She opened the door all huffy and shit. I told her what you said and I guess she didn't like it because next thing I know she's waving a gun around. I tried to get the hell outta there and this crazy bitch just shot me."

I looked over at Rossi to see if she was going to defend herself.

She had her head back on the chair, eyes closed. Yep, one crazy ass bitch. She's in a room with four armed men, well three and a half, and what does she do? She fucking feigns sleep.

"Hey Rossi are we boring you here?"

"Oh is the performance over, I'm sorry." she pretended to wipe sleep from her eyes while fake yawning.

This fucking chick.

"You have anything to say to this?"

"I already told you my version king Solomon, now it's up to you to decide who's telling the truth, but if there's any splitting in two to be done, I say cut Jimmy's other butt cheek make it all even."

"How bout I cut your fucking..."

"James for the last time, shut the fuck up, and you, stop with the bullshit and answer me. Do you have anything to say? It's only fair that a man gets to face his accuser."

"I knew you wouldn't believe me." she folded her arms in a huff, now she was acting like a brat who didn't get her way.

"I didn't say I didn't believe you."

"Shane..." I gave James a look to shut him the fuck up. I knew she was telling me the truth but I needed her to say it in front of him. The lying fuck.

"It's like I told you, he tried to grab my ass and I pretended to go into the bedroom to change into slut wear, as if." She sneered at him while turning up her nose like he was something foul.

"I came out with my gun, he had his pants halfway off by the time I got back and when he saw the gun he tried to run and I shot him. Now genius, if you were standing at the door, why were your pants off, second, why is there no bullet hole in your pants?"

She had a point that could easily be verified. I turned to look at him to see how he would try to weasel himself out of this one.

He looked like a fluttering fish that had gone too far on the sand and couldn't get back to the water.

"Well she tried to..."

"Stop lying James it's embarrassing. Tell me why I shouldn't cap your ass right fucking now?"

"I'm family..."

He started with the same bullshit excuse he always fell back on when he fucked up.

"Yeah, family who I sent on an errand in my name and you accosted a young woman while doing business IN MY MOTHERFUCKING NAME." I was yelling by the time I was through. He stepped the fuck back while Tony and Mikey stepped up to flank him, ready to do whatever I asked.

"Okay hood rats, calm down boys, the boy is green and horny, that's no reason to kill him. I'm thinking the shot to the ass is punishment enough for his troubles. Just keep him away from me and maybe he'll live to see his next birthday."

I just looked at her, now she was telling me how to run my shit.

"Get out of here James; I'll deal with you later."

As the fuck was leaving he looked back over his shoulder at me with a puppy dog look on his face.

"Don't tell ma okay?"

Fuck, no respect.

"Get the fuck outta here before I blow out your kneecaps."

He hobbled as fast as he could, yeah I might think twice about killing him, but there's nothing stopping me from maiming his dumb ass.

"Right, looks like I'm done here, can I go now?"

"I thought you wanted to see your new apartment and where you'll be working."

"What, now?"

"Why not, you got something better to do?"

Or someone maybe, I'm sure she had to have men falling all over her gorgeous ass. Once you got past that mouth of hers the rest of the package was spectacular.

"Okay, if you're sure let me go up and get my bag and stuff."

"Sure go ahead." What the fuck, I had shit lined up to do for the rest of the day, I didn't have time to be chauffeuring her around. But I wasn't quite ready to leave her company.

She left the room, that hot ass of hers hugged sweetly in those tight as fuck jeans, damn. I almost licked my lips.

"You better check her bag when she comes back bro." This was Mikey's suggestion as if I was too green to know that.

"Thanks for the info."

"That bad?"

"Tony man you have no idea, she makes our wives look like amateurs."

Tony whistled between his teeth.

"I think our bro here is in for a hell of a time, it'll be fun to see who comes out on top in this little war they got going on."

"Shut the fuck up Mikey, you two pussy whipped mother fuckers are just sad, watch and learn boys, watch and learn." The fucks fell all over themselves laughing. Fuckers.

"I want someone on her from now on."

"Any particular reason?" Tony asked.

'Because it's what I want, better make it Tommy."

Tommy was one of my best men, the woman was more trouble than she was worth, somehow I don't think I'm the only one she gets mouthy with, whatever she'd done before today was out of my control, but from now on I'll look out for her until I didn't feel the need to do it anymore. Which could be never.

Whatever! I never questioned myself or second-guessed my instincts. Right now they were screaming at me to keep 'mouth' close. So that's what I'll do. What the fuck will come of it was anyone's guess.

"Let's roll Tony Montana." She bounced back into the room.

I might end up killing her before the day was out, save myself the fucking headache.

Chapter 4

I have no idea how the fuck we ended up at my building. I had no intentions on moving her into my high rise, but for some fucked up reason we ended up here, on my floor, at a fifteen thousand dollar a month pad at one of the best addies in the fucking city if not the state.

I had to glare the two fuckwads better known as my brothers in law into submission since they were finding this shit funny. Probably thought I was becoming as whipped as their sorry asses. Fuck if I'd ever let that happen, especially not by some slip of a girl with trots of the mouth.

"What're we doing here?"

"I thought you wanted to see your new place?"

"Your cheese fall off your cracker Don Corleone?"

"Say what now." I knew this bitch was touched, what the fuck was she talking about, cheese and crackers?

"You hungry?" I looked at her perplexed.

"You're not too bright are you Shane?"

"How bout I clock you in that mouth of yours, would you like that?"

She batted her fucking eyes at me. Just once one little tap right across that mouth of hers, it would go a long way to assuaging my damn aggravation.

"Now what the fuck were you saying?"

"Never mind Rocky, but seriously dude, this place must cost a mint, I paid three fifty a month in rent, there's no way I can afford the rent on this place, are you bent?"

"Didn't I say you'd have the same deal, and stop with the insults before I really pop you one."

Ma would understand, she was always preaching to me about stress and shit, I just had to tell her the mouth was stressing me the fuck out, yeah that'll work.

"What's the catch, I mean how do you see me paying this off?"

"You're really obsessed with me fucking you aren't you mouth?"

"Whatever Tiny." she walked off.

Did she just insult my dick?

"You two shut the fuck up." Snickering fucks, I should shoot one of them just for the hell of it that ought to shut them both the hell up. Maybe not, then I'd have to deal with one of my crazy ass sisters. Fucking women.

"Are you always this difficult?" I followed her over to the wall of windows with a view over the city skyline

"Only when I'm being played."

"No one's playing you, this is one of my buildings, I never said where your new place was gonna be, why can't it be here, don't you think you deserve to be in a place like this?"

I thought I saw a softening of her lips.

"When I've earned it yes, until then sayonara." She headed for the door.

"Get back here you infuriating woman."

"What?"

Way too much attitude in this one.

"Listen, there's no catch okay, it's just that you're a young girl alone in the city. I have two sisters, if either one of them was in your position I would want someone to look out for them. Sure I could put you somewhere else, but this is the best I could come up with, it's secure, in the best neighborhood in our fine city and it's close to the club you'll be working at."

Quick thinking there Flanagan that sisters angle was fucking inspired, plus total bullshit, those two crazy broads could take down a motherfucker with sheer bitchiness alone.

Just let her buy this shit so I can get her moved in as soon as possible.

What about after you've fucked her and grown tired of her as you inevitably always do?

I'll cross that fucking bridge when I get to it. She can be moved out as easily as she's moved in.

I've never put a woman up in one of my places before, this was new territory for me, besides I wasn't exactly setting her up, she would be paying rent, pittance though it was.

"You sure that's all there is to it? There's no secret passage leading from your lair to me, no midnight visits in the dark. I sleep with my nine homes, just saying."

"Have a lot of experience with midnight visits do you?"

"Not really no, but since it looks like my caliber of acquaintance is about to change for the worse a girl can never be too careful."

Did she just...?

"Did you just insult me again?"

"Who, lil ole me nevah."

I needed this shit? What the fuck, my life wasn't fucked enough with fucking turf wars and takeover attempts; I had to add this shit to the mix? Fuck.

"You want the place or not?"

"Of course I want it, but I want a contract in writing that states my nookie is not for sale Repeat, Arianna Rossi's nookie is not up for grabs."

I held the bridge of my nose between my fingers where I felt the headache starting.

"You're fucking insane you know that?"

"You want my apartment over the pub?"

"I could always drop your ass in the river; I'm thinking that might be doing a lot of people a favor. In fact I should take out an ad in the paper see if a mother-fucker would pay me to take you out."

"You're horny aren't you?"

"What the fuck?"

"It's the only explanation for your crankiness, either that or not enough bran in your breakfast cereal, come on then time's a wasting, let's go look at my new place of employment Don Vito."

This chick watched way too much TV. I was constantly having to glare at the two stooges who seemed to think everything out of her mouth was funny, the fucks.

Chapter 5

What am I doing; seriously, I'm going to take her to my club where I spend most of my time.

Out of all my businesses this one was my favorite hangout, now she'll be living down the hall from me, right fucking next door, and she'll be here in my face, there'll be no fucking escape. It's official; I've lost my fucking mind.

"Let's go."

I took her elbow and was surprised when she didn't pull away right away.

My club is called Spice, it has three levels with bar, lounge and night club, each floor had textured walls in differing shades of blue from aqua to midnight blue, there were liquid floors on all three levels, the space had the capacity for three thousand and was usually full on the weekends with lines around the block. Mouth was sure to do good here if she didn't get herself killed; there are some pretty rough customers who liked to hang out in my place.

My head manager was waiting for us when we arrived since I'd called ahead and had her meet us here.

The place wouldn't be opened for business for a few hours yet, but there were staff members milling about getting things situated, I ran a tight mother-fucking ship and they knew not to fuck around.

"Teresa Ricci, Arianna Rossi, she'll be working the floor starting tomorrow night, get Jess to show her the ropes, show her around, explain shit. She has experience so it should just be a matter of learning the menus and how we do things around here."

I have no idea what happened between those two when Teresa showed her around, I was busy looking over the place, but as soon as they came back and Teresa moved off mouth was back in effect.

"Fucked that didn't you, you dog?" She sneered at me.

What the fuck?

"Why do you say that?"

"Because she gave me the death ray glare. Somehow I pegged you as having better taste than that. She looks like a poodle having a fucked up hair day."

Okay I couldn't gut the guys for laughing at that one, that was kinda funny, but damn, new dilemma.

Oh shit, maybe this wasn't such a good idea after all, mouth had no filter and Teresa was trying to get back on my dick, not gonna happen.

But I was for damn sure gonna try getting into mouth's snatch first chance I get, which might cause a problem with the two of them working in such close proximity.

"Well come on Luca Brasi I have to go pack."

"Would you stop with the Godfather shit already?"

"Whatever you say Santino, say bye to the happy hooker and let's be out.

Oh yeah, this had shit storm written all over it.

Chapter 6

In one week mouth has managed to alienate most of her co workers, except the guys, they of course loved her, the girls, not so much.

I got more complaints in the last few days than in the whole time that I've had this place. There was name calling, put downs and what some called just plain rude.

To hear it from the guys behind the bar and the kitchen staff, it was a different story, they couldn't sing her praises enough, and beyond that, two things.

The customers loved the shit out of her, both men and women and she was a fucking selling machine.

She sold more top shelf shit in one night than most of my girl's sold in a week. She was making money for my place and from evidenced by the tips on her credit card slips she wasn't doing too badly herself.

So my conclusion: jealousy.

Don't get me wrong I know mouth is a pain in the ass, I heard her ask Vivienne if she was dropped on her head at birth because apparently one of Vivienne's regulars decided he wanted to sit in mouth's section one night and Vivienne thought she should still get to take him. He was a big tipper apparently.

The bus boys all had her back, they snitched to me about some of the shit that some of the others tried to pull on her but my girl didn't take anybody's shit as they all soon found out.

Teresa was the worst complainant of the bunch, nothing Ari did seemed good enough for her ass, and it didn't take a rocket scientist to figure that one out.

I was ready to tell all of them to leave me the fuck alone, because I wasn't getting rid of her no matter what the fuck they said.

The only one not complaining was mouth; she never said shit to me about anything. Stubborn as shit.

Tommy said she was the easiest job he had he was bored already.

She went to school, came home, went to work, and came home. What the fuck he did while she was in class was anybody's guess, as long as he kept her safe and out of trouble I could give a fuck.

Tonight I'm sitting in the V.I.P lounge, there're a few other tables in there that I let some of my closer acquaintances use from time to time. I didn't sit with those fucks though, when I was in my place I sat with my crew so I could keep an eye on shit.

That fucker James Foster was in my place tonight, which meant I had to be on my mother fucking Ps and Qs, that fuck was crazy on a good day and homicidal on the rest.

He also fancied himself a pretty boy and a lady's man, guess there were no mirrors in his fucked up world.

I should've known there was going to be trouble when I saw Ari coming up to the lounge to go to their table, now James was no acquaintance of mine, but his boss Jonathan was cool people, some of my other associates didn't like dealing with him because of the color of his skin, asked me how I could do business with him, I told them because the only color I saw was motherfucking green, bigoted fucks.

Mouth isn't supposed to work the lounge, only seasoned workers worked this section, you had to earn that privilege so why the fuck was Teresa sending her up here to Foster's table no less?

The first time she went to the table I held my fucking breath like a little bitch.

Things seemed to go well, she walked away to go fill their orders and they were laughing and joking, all except Jonathan who wasn't looking too happy, I couldn't hear what the fucks were saying from two tables over, but I saw the looks.

That fucker James was licking his lips like he was at a meal while watching her ass in her black mini skirt. Try it and die mother- fucker.

My boys sensed my tension and went on alert, I didn't know what the fuck was about to go down but I was ready for whatever the fuck jumped off.

She came back with a tray of drinks.

I saw his intent before he put thought into action and was out my chair in a flash a bottle of Dom in hand, he grabbed her ass, and I brought the bottle down across the back of his mother-fucking head.

Mikey and Tony were there before I could follow through.

I looked at Jonathan.

"He never steps foot in my mother-fucking place again."

I grabbed her hand, gave my boys orders to clean up this shit and throw that fuck out back with the rest of the trash.

"Slow your roll there Nicky Scarfo." she tried to free her hand but I just kept going.

"What did I tell you about that shit?"

"Hey that's not from the Godfather; he's a whole other breed of crazy."

"Shut up mouth before I shut you up."

"Make me."

So I did, right there in the middle of my motherfucking club for the whole world to see, I picked her little ass up and kissed the fuck outta her.

That ought a keep her ass quiet for two seconds.

Chapter 7

Oh my, he's a caveman mobster, that kiss had my hoo-hah weeping, shit he was all kinds a good. Damn if I'd let him know though.

I slid down his body when he was finished assaulting my mouth, good thing he grabbed me again because my knees were shot.

He led me upstairs to his office, poured me a cognac and sat behind his desk.

"What's this?"

"Drink it."

I shrugged my shoulders whatever, that shit burned like a mother-fucking bitch.

"Who was that jackass you tried to decapitate Tommy Pitera?"

"What the fuck do you do study the mob or some shit?"

"Among other things."

"To answer your question pain in the ass his name's James Foster."

"Another one, what the fuck is up with these James guys and my ass?"

"There's a difference, my little brother is a twenty year old kid who doesn't know his head from his ass, this asshole is a mean, vicious piece a shit."

"Gotcha he's a whole other brand a cray, cray, okey dokey."

"What were you doing up there anyway, I thought that was Dina's section tonight."

"Your girlfriend told me to go, I don't think Dina was too happy about it though and to tell you the truth if only pigs hang out up there I'd rather keep my section thank you very much." she batted her eyes at me.

"You think I don't know you just insulted me don't you?" She tried to look innocent and shit, yeah right.

"So how's it going so far?"

"It's going great, it will be even better when you let me get back out there so I can make some money."

"You're not going back on the floor tonight."

"Excuse me, why not? it's Friday night, one of the best nights for tips, no can do Louis lump, lump." I headed for the door but he caught me around my middle and dragged me onto his lap.

"That better be a gun in your pocket."

"It's my dick; now sit still before I introduce you."

Just for kicks I gave a little grind on his goods, that'll teach him. Maybe not his mouth was on mine again and I was swallowing his tongue.

Chapter 8

It's back to work for me, I haven't seen the boss yet since I arrived maybe I'll get lucky and he'll stay out of my business.

“What the fuck, mouth what're you doing?”

Oops spoke too soon.

Apparently that James guy hadn't cashed in his ticket last night; good for him, I had more important things to deal with right now than his stupid ass.

I have to deal with this crazy ass man who seems to think he could tell me what to do. Uh huh that's gonna work.

"I'm working the floor."

"No! You're not."

'Why not?" Oh he wanted to clip me one, instead he was back to pulling out his hair or at least giving a good impression of it.

"Were you not there when that fucking asshole grabbed your ass?"

"Oh please Copernicus, guys have been grabbing my ass since forever..."

"What the fuck, who?" He looked ready to commit murder.

I just gave him a look, he was mental, then again all mobster types usually were, at least that's my take.

"Never mind all that, I have to get back on the floor. You kept me off last night, apparently so you could get off, how'd that work out for you?" I smirked at him, this guy was so easy to work up, just call him a few names, ignore a couple of his dictates and he was ready to strangle me, sheesh, like now, he was looking at me like he wanted to chuck me out the window, hah.

See, I knew she was going to drive me fucking crazy, bat shit just like she is. She'd tried to bite off my tongue last night, crazy nut. Like she hadn't enjoyed it.

I know she'd been enjoying it just fine until the fucking guys knocked on the door; I'll be ready for her later though.

"I don't need your ass on the fucking floor, how many mother-fuckers you want me to have to kill?"

"Oh my! The light's on but nobody's home." She shook her head like I was a lost cause or some shit.

"Say what now."

"Nothing, nothing, just talking to myself."

"Do that a lot do ya?"

"What's it to ya, now back to business, I'm going back to the floor and you can't stop me, I have rights you know. If you're so worried about it tell your patrons to keep their filthy hands to themselves, not just me, but all the girls."

Like I give a fuck about all the girls, some of them encouraged that shit, though I didn't want that shit in my place. I don't peddle flesh, ma would scalp my ass, 'nough said.

What the fuck am I gonna do with crazy chick, couldn't she understand that I would've killed that fucker last night if my boys hadn't pulled me off of him? The next motherfucker might not get off so easy.

"How about behind the bar?"

"Don't know shit about mixing drinks."

"I know! You can work on the books."

"You been dropped on your head one time too many. I, am, going, back, on, the, floor." She folded her arms after giving me shit.

Oh hell, I knew I should never have brought her here, now I'll never get any work done worrying about somebody's hands on her ass. Fuck me.

"Fine, go on the floor, but if I end up killing a mother-fucker it's on you."

"Oh yeah, who're the other hundred or so on Bugsy Siegel?"

This fucking girl!

"Get to work will ya?"

She flounced off in her little skirt and tight top, she was going to drive me up the fucking wall, I just knew it.

I watched her for a while on camera, everything seemed cool, I had Dom one of the bouncers on her from afar and they all knew if anything jumped off involving her they were to call me.

What they thought of that edict I didn't know and didn't give a fuck.

I finally got some work done since pain in the ass seemed to be staying out of trouble so far.

At around three in the morning, which was closing time I had Mikey go get her and bring her up to my office. There was no sense in her taking a cab when we were going to the same place.

She came through the door huffing and puffing while pulling off her shoes.

"My dogs aren't barking, they've crawled into a hole and died." She dropped down on the couch.

"Dogs, what dogs, you're not allowed to have dogs in my building."

They all started laughing, her, Mikey and Tony.

"What the fuck's so funny?"

"It's an expression moron, it means my feet hurt." She rolled her eyes at me like I was fucking stupid.

"Why the fuck didn't you just say that shit, the fuck you keep talking in riddles, I look like I have time to decipher code. If your feet hurt sit down, put them up and I'll take you home soon.

"You're such a sweetheart, how can I resist?"

One clip to the chin, please just one, who could blame me really, crazy ass nut job. Dogs barking and shit, and those two assholes weren't any better, laughing their fucking heads off, the fucks.

We were halfway home when the attack happened, they came at us from all sides, guns blazing, stupid fucks as if I'd let them corner me.

Two cars tried to box us in; one in front and one behind, what they didn't know was that I always had a trailer a few cars back for situations just like this, not to mention the only thing piercing this fucking tank on wheels is a drone.

I still pulled her head down just to be safe, while my guys took charge. My driver could outmaneuver Andretti on a bad day, no fear, just drive right through those fucks, they weren't expecting that shit, they expected us to try to evade fuck that shit.

I had the phone to my ear and my other hand on her head holding her down even though nothing was getting through my shit, but you never know.

"Who?"

I got the answer and hung up, I guess the fucks wanted a war after all.

"Who?" Mikey asked.

"Stacco."

If I had been paying closer attention I would've noticed the sudden tension in Arianna's body.

Chapter 9

My guys pulled into the underground parking garage beneath my building after my security detail ascertained it hadn't been breached.

My would be attackers were roasting their nuts up on the boulevard, good luck with identifying them.

I pulled mouth out the car behind me; she seemed no worse for wear for all that she'd been shot at.

Crazy lady was acting like it was par for the course.

I appeared calm on the outside, but inside I was coldly furious. Stacco was a dead fuck. He'd played his hand and lost, amateur fucker.

"You doing okay there mouth?" I checked her over more closely to make sure she wasn't in shock or some shit.

"Oh just peachy, tell me again why it makes more sense for me to catch a ride with you than taking a cab? If I knew I would be trying out for a part in A Bronx tale, I would've dressed more appropriately."

Did I say this bitch was crazy, certifiable?

Where were the tears and recriminations, the screaming and accusations? Why wasn't she screaming nine one one like any rational woman would be?

"You're coming home with me." We were on our way up in the elevator.

I pulled her to my door when we reached our floor, there was no way I was letting her out of my sight.

For some fucking reason I was more worried about her safety than my own. If they'd fucking hurt her I would've hunted the fuckers down and killed them with my bare hands.

As it was I planned on going after them as soon as fucking possible, the father and the fucking son, I'm going to obliterate the whole fucking family 'til there was none of those fucks left.

"I'm thinking hanging with you might be detrimental to my health. I don't fare so good when messing with you Lucky Luciano."

"Do you ever shut the fuck up?"

"Yep, when I'm alone in my own place, which is exactly where I'll be in one, two, three."

I pulled her through the fucking door and kissed the fuck outta her, it was the only way I knew of to shut her the fuck up. Plus, I needed it.

I had her up against the wall, her legs wrapped around me as I ground my hard on into her softness. I knew I was past the point of no return, I knew this is exactly where I wanted us to end up since that first day in my office, I just thought it would take me longer to get her on board.

Adrenaline pumped through me like a force field, I ravaged her mouth as I tore her panties from her body and got my pants opened, I didn't hear stop so I kept going. She was already wet for me, which made me groan into her mouth with appreciation.

I pushed into her body and got stopped cold; my mind couldn't quite process what my body was feeling.

"Fuck me, you're kidding right?"

"Surprise." She was as gone as I was, her hands in my hair; nails digging into my scalp, made me want to devour her.

"It's too late, I can't stop." My hips thrust against hers again and again.

"Who asked you to De Sade?"

That fucking mouth.

She'd screamed when I breached her.

Untouched and I'd taken her like a rutting animal, up against the fucking wall, no finesse, but that's what she did to me.

She drove me over the edge. I tried to go easy, bring some tenderness into the game but no dice, I was too far gone to pull back, I could only try to bring her along with me by touching her with my fingers right where she needed me to.

She squeezed down on me and my fucking knees almost buckled.

"That's right baby, take what you need from me."

She felt better than anything I had ever experienced before in my life: soft, hot, wet and all mine.

This changed everything, she was never getting away from me now; there was no way I was giving up this treasure.

Fuck, I knew she was going to be trouble.

She's asleep, I wore the poor girl out, who knew that virgin pussy would be that addictive? It was like I couldn't get enough of her body.

After that first time I'd had her in the shower, in the living room on the couch and then again in bed before sleep claimed us.

With all the fucking going on there was no time for questions thank heaven and her mouth had been otherwise occupied so she couldn't keep throwing names of gangsters at me in between insults. She was a real piece of work.

A fucking virgin, who the fuck would ever believe that shit, with that mouth of hers it was hard to grasp, well no one else would ever have to wonder about it because no other mother-fucker was ever getting near her, I'd kill them both.

I stamped my claim on that shit last night, the only thing I didn't do was brand the shit with a branding iron, and I couldn't wait to hit it again this morning either.

I'd taken care of her afterwards, I'm not a complete animal, I knew she would have a little discomfort after the way I kept after her so I'd given her a nice hot bath and rubbed some salve inside her to help ease the sting, she should be nice and ready for me when she finally woke up. If I could wait that long.

"Come on mouth wake up." I bit her ear lightly, of course crazy lady couldn't act like any other rational woman after a night of hot sex, no she came up swinging, almost caught me a good one too.

"Easy there slugger it's just me."

She seemed confused for all of one minute before the fog seemed to clear, before she could come completely to her senses and start talking at me I slid home.

Sweet, soft, lush, damn, had anything ever felt this good around my dick before, I don't remember it. I took her mouth in a deep kiss as our bodies danced together.

I hadn't realized how small she was before, she had such a big fucking mouth I forgot she was just a mere five two or three, I towered over her in the bed, but it didn't matter, the relevant parts fit perfectly.

I don't think I'd ever been this close to another human being in my life, it felt as though I needed to draw her into me, her legs clutched at me as her nails dug into my back and ass.

I could do this shit all day, if I wasn't careful she'd have me just as whipped as those two fucks Mikey and Tony, and I really didn't need to be thinking about how they got that way at this moment in time.

"Cum Arianna." I bit into her neck as I ground myself against her little love nub sending her into paroxysms of ecstasy. We both cried out from the pleasure as I emptied myself inside her.

It was time to talk, there were some things that had to be put on the table, not least of all was the fact that she now belonged to me, I had no doubt she'd try to fight me on that but it didn't matter, my mind was made up, she gave me her virginity, I held that shit in high regard,

I was gonna put a ring on it like the song said, first chance I get even if I have to hog tie her ass and get her to the church. I fully expected it to come to that, which means I'm just as fucked in the head as she is.

I cornered her in the bath tub, I'd run us a nice hot bath with some sea side smelling bath salts, she was quiet this morning and I wondered if that was a regular occurrence or just her natural shyness after last night and this morning.

Hopefully this was her norm in the mornings at least then I was sure to get some peace and quiet out of some part of the day.

"So Machiavelli you've deflowered little old me, what do you plan to do with me now, toss me aside like yesterday's news?"

"I plan to drag your ass in front of a priest as soon as my ma can arrange that shit." That got your attention. She sat up like something stung her on the ass.

"Are you on something, you do know crack kills right?"

Yeah, I wanted to spend the next fifty years listening to this shit, like I didn't have enough of this shit when I was a kid, surrounded by crazy ass women. Shit can you imagine Sunday dinners at the house, damn, her and my two sisters together, that almost scared me more than being shot at.

I chose to ignore her question since we were getting hitched with or without her consent.

"So, who all was shooting at you last night, a disgruntled husband perchance?" she had the nerve to bat her fucking lashes at me.

"I don't poach on other people's territory how insulting."

"Don't get your panties in a bunch there Shawna baby, sheesh."

I should just drown her now save myself the fucking aggravation.

"Wasn't no Shawna that popped that cherry babe."

Oh fuck the mouth could blush, get the fuck out, she was pulling her hair into her face to hide it. Well well well looks like I finally found a way to shut her up.

"Any way to answer your question it's nothing for you to worry about, they were after me, I doubt they even know who you are. They'll be dealt with soon enough anyway so put it out of your head.

"Sure, why don't I just forget the whole thing, you said something about Stacco, is that the name of a person or a paint job?"

"It's Stacco not stucco, stucco is a binder used..."

"Yeah I really need a lesson in decorative house art from you right now Professor X."

“Did you just call me a mutant?"

"If the green fits baby...hey..."

I pulled her under water by her feet, she came up spluttering and I'm sure ready for battle.

"Settle the fuck down will ya, damn it's too fucking early for this shit, now forget everything you heard last night, that's the end of it."

"You're a poor demented soul aren't you, bless your heart?"

I could only sigh and close my eyes to escape the insanity that was my life.

"Anyway, I need to go home at some point because I can't work in the same clothes as last night."

"My wife isn't working in no fucking club are you bent."

"You be sure and tell that poor beleaguered woman I send my condolences, now back to me and my need for clean clothes."

I threw the washcloth at her fucking head.

"Oh thank you." She started washing her arms with it.

What am I gonna do with this woman; she'll have me in an early grave faster than my enemy's bullet.

Needless to say we spent the rest of the day arguing until I got frustrated enough to lock her in the bedroom with no way out. You can imagine the curses that were heaped on my head.

"You do realize you just cursed your own firstborn son don't you, since the only sons I will be having will be coming from you."

She tried to scream the fucking place down after that.

"Having trouble there boss, you need a hand with that?"

"Why don't you see to your own affairs and leave mine alone Mikey, you jerk?"

"Just trying to be helpful bro, you ready to go to work or you need some more time with the little lady?"

"Let's go and shut the fuck up."

"Seriously though man, congratulations."

"What the fuck are you talking about?"

"Dude that little lady is so your wife."

"What do you mean?"

"Dude where the fuck have you been she's had you going in circles the last few weeks, I've known you damn near our whole lives and I've never seen you so gone over a chick before."

What the fuck, he couldn't be right, could he, nah, I was just marrying mouth out of honor, it was the right thing to do after taking her virginity, it's what ma would expect. That's right I'm doing it for ma. I could live with that, Mikey was a douche he didn't know what the fuck he was talking about.

"What are you a fucking old woman, let's get the fuck outta here before mouth breaks out and fucks us both up."

"Bro you can't leave her in there all night."

"I know that you ass, I plan on coming back early after I know what the fuck is going on with the search for Stacco."

He started humming some shit under his breath and shaking his head at me.

"What?"

"Nothing."

"Then shut the fuck up."

"Didn't say a word bro."

“Then stop thinking whatever you're thinking so fucking loud."

"Damn bro, she's rubbing off on you already."

“You better run you fuck." He dodged the blow I threw at his head and ran to the elevator, just what I needed; now him and the other one would be yakking my fucking ears off all day about this shit.

Chapter 11

I tried the key in the door with as much trepidation as one facing a firing squad.

I knew she was going to be pissed all the fuck off, who knows what crazy lady had in store for me.

I opened the door to complete quiet, not a sound, I walked down the long ass hallway and got my first surprise, my bedroom door was standing open.

My heart started racing out of my fucking chest, where the fuck was she? My head started doing some buzzing shit and I felt like I was about to black the fuck out.

If my enemies had gotten to her, if they had harmed one hair on her fucking head I'm going to turn this motherfucking city into a river of blood.

It was then I heard a noise coming from the kitchen and drew my gun.

I'd let Mikey and Tony go because all they were doing was getting on my fucking nerves, humming the fucking wedding march and shit.

I crept down the hallway, gun at the ready until I reached the kitchen.

This fucking girl, what was I gonna do with her?

"Easy there quick draw McGraw."

"Mouth what the fuck!"

She was sitting at the kitchen table eating a feast; I had to sit down before my legs gave out.

"How'd you get out?" I put my gun away; then again I probably should keep it at the ready in case she decided to retaliate.

"Wouldn't you like to know, I think I'll keep that knowledge to myself just in case you decide to lose your damn mind again, just so you know I'm only letting this one slide because you were looking out for my safety, do it again and I'll have your balls capisce!"

"Whatever mob girl." The way she was holding that sausage looked ominous, when she chopped piece off I cringed, crazy bitch, she probably would too.

I got up and walked around behind her, my hands automatically drawn to her boobs.

"Eating here horn dog, besides that ship has sailed, been there done that."

"My ass." I bit her neck, she couldn't resist that shit that was her weakness, the long drawn out moan told me I hit my mark.

"Make it quick I got work." She pushed back her chair, faced me and attacked my mouth, I had her on the kitchen island and was inside her before she could form another thought.

Damn I'd missed her, I hadn't even been gone that long, she was grabbing me with her inner walls as I laid her back for a better angle.

Her legs went around my neck, my hands on her nipples, she bit her damn lip and I got hot as fuck.

"That's fucking hot baby." She wasn't paying me any mind; she was too busy enjoying what I was doing to her.

I didn't last too long but I made sure she got hers too.

"Gotta go."

What the fuck?

"Where're you going?"

"Gotta get some stuff at my place, isn't your security on the job, it should be safe."

She had a point but I still didn't want her going over there without me, oh well it was only next door no problem.

She was gone entirely too long, what the hell did she need to get, I thought she went to get clothes, I got caught up trying to find her the perfect ring design of all things, what! I wasn't going soft; she would be wearing the damn thing for the rest of her life the least I could do was make sure it was something she would like.

Just as I was about to go fetch her the in house phone rang.

"Yeah."

"Uh, boss, I wasn't sure if I should call or not she did say you said it was okay..."

What the fuck had she done now?

"What is it?" I rubbed my forehead where I felt a headache coming on.

"Well she just left..."

"She did what?" There goes my heart again, was she trying to fucking kill me?"

By the time I found my keys and was heading for the door not knowing where the fuck I was going my cell rang. The fucking club, what could they want now; I'd been there already.

"It's me."

"I thought you said she wasn't working here anymore!"

"Ricci?"

"Yes, your protégé is here and she says you said it's okay, I don't know what the hell is going on but I'm the manager here and I need to be kept in the loop."

I hung up on her ass, I know that bitch wasn't about to threaten me, I went out the door calling the brothers Grimm as I went, if I went anywhere without them they would gripe like two bitches, and then they would get ma on me, fucking yentas.

They met me outside the club grins on their stupid faces, oh shit.

"Ma."

"Hi son, I came to meet my new daughter." She was all smiles; I gave the two blabbermouths that were standing with their wives my best 'you're dead motherfuckers look.'

Fuckers laughed at me.

We turned and headed inside, I'm not sure I was ready for this meet and greet. Fuck.

Chapter 12

Ma lead the way into the noisy club, looking around with a smile on her face, like she knew what mouth looked like.

Then again with these two ya yas she probably knew down to my girls' shoe size. Big mouthed fucks.

Wait till I get them alone, they had the good sense to stick close to their wives.

I don't fuck with my sisters, you ever seen a pissed off feral cat, well tie two of them together in a sack and you have Anna and Sophia, and that's on a good day.

Teresa came over all gushing smiles.

"Hello Mrs. Flanagan, so nice of you to join us this evening."

"Hello Teresa, how are you dear?"

Mom is a diplomat down to her toes, she hated it when she suspected I was banging Teresa, I had to keep reassuring her that I had no intention of marrying the other woman, that she was just a distraction, no matter what she thought.

Mom had to be satisfied with that, I'm a man after all, I had needs. Imagine the embarrassment of discussing that shit with your mother.

I saw mouth laughing it up with this table of about seven men, of course no women.

They were all smiling and ogling her tits and ass, probably imagining getting her naked! Like fuck.

If those assholes knew what was good for them they'd keep their fucking eyes to themselves.

She didn't see us as Ricci lead us upstairs to my family's lounge. Ma had a private lounge in all my places.

Most of my clubs and restaurants were two years old or younger, those I'd built separate from the business granddad had passed down to me.

His shit was import export, oil, high end luxury goods and shit like that.

The clubs and restaurants were legit, I was trying to get all my businesses on the up and up but that shit was easier said than done.

Plus I liked fucking with the law. Corrupted fucks, some of those bastards made me look like a choir boy.

When we were seated and Teresa was still futilely trying to get into my mother's good graces, ma pulled out the big guns.

"So where's this new daughter of mine Shane, please don't tell me you have the poor girl working, that will never do. Bring her here to me."

Teresa almost shit herself, her face turned red as fuck and she was fuming, I guess she knew who ma was referring to.

She kept that shit inside because she knew better than to mouth off at ma, I would seriously cap her ass right here if the bitch even tried, no one fucked with ma, not now not ever.

"Bring Ari up here will ya."

"She's busy with a table." She tried giving me attitude like that shit was gonna fly.

"Pass it off to Dina or one of the others, just get her up here."

I dismissed her.

The girls were all excited and shit, and made me wonder what the fuck Mutt and Jeff had told

them about me and mouth, apparently they'd told them enough to have ma coming downtown late at night.

"Where's dad?"

"He'll be here, he was in the middle of something when the boys dropped by."

These two fucks; so here's the deal.

My family has an estate that's acres and acres of fucking Flanagan land as far as the eye can see and beyond.

Anna and Tony built their home there, so did Sophie and Mikey, and of course ma and dad live in the original Flanagan mansion this big old monster that dates back to the seventeen hundreds or some shit.

Ma insisted that my family home be there as well and since I make it a point never to fuck with ma, there is where it is, though I spend most of my time at my condo

The shit's more suited to a family, I'm a bachelor, at least I was until about twenty hours ago.

Anyway, having everyone so close together didn't leave room for secrets ya know, and ma liked to be kept in the loop, especially when it came to me.

"Where's James?"

"He wasn't feeling too well, I don't know what is going on with that boy, he's been hiding out in his room the last couple weeks."

What happened is that your new daughter put a cap in his ass and he can't tell you that because then he'd have to explain why.

Mouth came up the stairs smiling, I don't know what Teresa told her, probably didn't warn her it was us.

I saw the smile fall off her face and wondered what the fuck was wrong now.

I got it one second before she flew over the table straight for my fucking throat. The fuck?

I pulled her hands away from my neck while Tony and Mikey tried to get her off me.

"Leave her."

I was looking into her eyes, so I saw the hurt and betrayal, and the sheen of tears forming. Good.

You see, the way we were sitting, three men, and three women, it looked all cozy and shit, not to mention ma looked like she could pass for thirty easy.

That's what mouth saw when she came up the stairs and drew the wrong conclusion.

"Ari, I'd like you to meet my mother Pia and my sisters, Sophia and Anna.

I felt the tension leave her body, only to return a second later.

"Oops, I'm guessing I couldn't go out and come back in again huh?"

"I don't think so babe."

Ma's mouth was hanging open, meanwhile my sisters were looking like they didn't know whether to laugh or take her down, though we were already on the floor.

When Tony and Mikey started laughing their asses off it broke the ice and I helped us both up off the ground, keeping my arms round her as I turned her to ma.

Ma was beaming, see she understood crazy, she'd given birth to enough of it, raised it, lived it, she knew crazy, crazy was right up her alley. I'm telling you, the woman is a saint.

"Well hello Arianna, that's quite an entrance you made there."

"I'm so sorry Mrs. Flanagan; I don't know what came over me."

"Of course you do, and I accept the compliment, you thought I was Shane's date didn't you?"

Uh...uhm....well...."

The mouth had no words, will wonders never cease.

"Don't give it a second thought dear, come sit here by me."

She walked over and sat between ma and Anna, with Sophia leaning over to get into the conversation.

"So Arianna tell us about yourself, I don't think I know anyone with the name of Rossi."

"I'm not from around here; I came from a small town here in Illinois."

"With your family?"

I was watching her closely which seemed to be all I ever did when in her company, so when she answered I saw the touch of sadness that entered her eyes.

"No ma'am, I don't really have any family left to speak of.

Yep, that was one sure fired way to have ma drag her off to the family home, ma loves a sad story.

"Well you do now, doesn't she girls?"

Of course they agreed, everyone agreed with ma if they knew what was good for them.

"Your skin is amazing."

"Thank you, Sophia right?"

"That's me, so how did you wind up with this freak anyway?"

"Uhm, we kinda just met I guess."

"That's not what I heard."

"Sophie kill that shit will ya' where're the drinks, did anybody order drinks?"

"I'm on it boss." Mikey got up to go get us some shit to drink, he knew what we liked.

"What about you Ari, what'll you have?" he asked before leaving.

"Ah, nothing! I'm working."

"No you're not, I fired you remember?"

"You can't fire me, on what grounds?"

"On the grounds that my wife does not work in my club."

"That's her problem not mine."

I can't pop her one in front of ma, that wouldn't be good, and the way my sisters were looking at her I was sure if I even tried they would probably gut me.

"Son looks like you've met your match; I don't see why Ari can't continue to work until the babies come."

Before I could respond mouth was heard from.

"She smoke bud too huh?"

Did she just imply that my mother was high?

I hung my head as the whole table erupted in laughter, what am I gonna do with this girl?"

"Well I have to go now; it was nice meeting you all."

"Mouth, you try to go back on that floor we got problems."

"Bring it John Dillinger."

I gave her a look, was she always going to make me crazy?

"Ma you seeing this shit?"

"She's just what you need; I think she's perfect, not like that other one."

She sniffed her nose in the direction Teresa had gone leaving no doubt as to whom she meant.

"Oh you mean the electrocuted poodle?"

"Oh shit, is that what you call Teresa, that's priceless." Anna high fived her.

Yep, I can just see my life unfolding before me, crazy all the way to the fucking grave, no let up.

I guess I deserve that shit for the life I lead.

I grabbed her from between ma and Anna and put her back next to me so she couldn't disobey me.

Heaven knows how she was gonna make me pay for that.

We spent the rest of the night with the women playing twenty questions, I had to hold onto mouth the whole night to get her to stay put, which wasn't really a hardship, I even managed to steal a kiss or two without losing any body parts.

This felt right, having her here with my family.

By the time dad came along the others had a nice buzz going, I was the only one not drinking, I liked knowing what the fuck was going on around me.

Teresa had tried to infiltrate once more but the unexplained eruption of laughter when she showed up soon had her running away again.

My sisters were mean bitches.

Dad fell in love with my girl of course; he claimed he had someone to side with him in our Sunday debates.

We left the club in the early morning hours, my girl had exchanged numbers with the family, she seemed a little hesitant but I chalked that up to her independent nature, she probably felt like she'd been sucked into a vortex. My family was fucking nuts. Except ma of course.

I had to wrestle her to my door since she was under the delusion that she was going to her place, she didn't know that the only time she was going back there was to get her stuff.

"Stop fucking around mouth you're staying here, with me."

As she opened her mouth to blast me again I just did what I always do to shut her up, I covered her mouth with mine.

She tried to bite me so I bit her lip first before taking her tongue while pushing my hand between her thighs.

"All night I've been waiting to get my hands on you."

I pushed pass her underwear and found her opening with my fingers. She moaned in my

mouth letting me know that she was enjoying this. Good maybe she won't tie my dick in a knot when I try to fuck her.

"I wanna fuck you so bad mouth, will you let me?"

For an answer she wrapped her leg around mine drawing me closer, my pants were in the way, couldn't have that.

I walked us backwards to the bedroom and over to the bed, all the while we were fighting each other with our mouths, she kept biting me and I her until one of us conquered the other with our tongue.

I didn't have the patience to get undressed all the way so I just unzipped, pulled my cock out, moved her panties to the side and pulled her down on me.

"Hmmm."

At least I found something that she liked.

"Ride my cock baby." She didn't really know what to do so I showed her what I liked. She was such a sensual being that she caught on quick.

Our kisses grew heated and almost violent as I fucked up into her with forceful thrusts. She grabbed my hair like she wanted to pull that shit out at the roots.

I think my girl liked rough play, only one way to find out.

I bit my way down her neck to her nipple, tearing her shirt from her body, she fucking came on my dick. Fuck.

"Damn baby your pussy is so fucking hot."

"Shane."

"Hmm, yes love."

"Shut up and fuck."

Fucking girl.

She's tearing at my clothes so I threw her on the bed to take them off. She reared up and bit my lip again while grabbing my cock trough my pants.

"I can't get them off if you don't let go babe."

"Then hurry up."

Now she was biting my chest, that shit made my boy stand up tall, when she pushed my pants off my hips and took me in her mouth, I thought I had died and gone to heaven.

What she lacked in expertise she more than made up for in eagerness.

Her nails were digging into my ass as she tried to get more of me in her mouth, I was hitting her throat and pulling back not wanting to hurt her, she wanted it all.

I leaned over her back and played with her ass since I couldn't reach her pussy from this angle.

I threw her back on the bed, laid on my back and pulled her over me so her pussy was right over my mouth.

She went fucking insane as I tongued her wet pussy while my nose rubbed her clit.

"Play with your tits baby." I pulled my tongue out long enough to order.

She pulled on her nipples while she rode my face.

Her pussy tasted sweet as fuck, I'd never tasted anything like it, virgin pussy.

I wasn't feeling very tender when I pushed her off my tongue and tried to mount her, but she had other ideas.

We grappled all over my king sized bed scratching and biting before I turned her over onto her hands and knees, bit into her neck and slid home forcefully burying my cock to the root.

"This is how a dominant animal mounts his mate."

I fucked deep, my teeth back in her neck keeping her in place like some wild animal.

She was still trying to fight me, I bit harder, again she creamed my meat.

My balls were slapping against her clit which seemed to be driving her crazy.

I played in her ass as I fucked her harder than I'd ever fucked anyone before.

"What are you doing to me......uhhhhh, that's so good, why is it so good?"

I manhandled her tits roughly I forced her hips lower to the bed, just like a wild fucking animal.

"You like it rough don't you mob girl?"

She bucked against me trying to throw me off but my dick was buried too deep inside her.

"That's right baby, fuck back on my dick." I kept whispering shit in her ear that just seemed to spur her on.

"I'm gonna fuck you hard every time you disobey me, next time I'm going to tie you to the fucking bed. Then I'm gonna beat your ass with my belt, no love taps either, until you learn to fucking listen."

Then I decided to fuck with her don't ask me why.

"You see who's going to be in charge from now on don't you little girl?"

"Fuck that, I want on top."

I slapped her ass hard. Oh I'll pay for that I'm sure.

"You get on top when I say, right now I want to show you who's boss, who owns you, owns your pussy from now on."

Now she was mad and my dick reaped the benefits.

She squeezed down on me almost making me come too soon; I pinched her nipples until she released me, and then gave her ass another slap for that shit.

"I've taken you down, mounted you and taken your pussy, what're you gonna do about it?"

She almost pulled off my dick but I grabbed her hips and pulled her back forcefully going even deeper than before. I saw fucking stars as I went past her cervix.

"Fuuuuuck, hold on to the sheets babe I'm about to fuck the shit outta you."

I piston my dick into her until the bed shook, every time I entered her cervix she grunted and her pussy twitched.

"Oh fuck Shane that feels so good, more more more, fuck me harder." She was totally gone, her only thoughts on her pussy and feeling good.

I lifted her right leg and sank my bone deeper into her pussy rubbing against her clit with every movement.

My cock was covered completely in her juices, the sounds coming out of our throats were not human and I couldn't stop.

Her nails were tearing the sheets to shreds as she screamed and came.

I pulled her hair and her head back so I could kiss her while I emptied my seed deep inside her womb.

She was riding out the last of her orgasm on my still hard dick, her pussy twitching and squeezing on me.

"Fuck mouth that was hot as fuck."

"Yeah, but next time I want to be on top."

"We'll see." At least she accepted that there would be a next time, if I had my way that would be in about another half hour or so.

I turned her over on her back and ate her pussy just to keep her primed while my shit got back to iron hardness.

She pulled my face into her pussy, wrapping her legs around my head, seems my girl liked to be fucked by my tongue.

I brought her to orgasm with my tongue and fingers three more times before mounting her again this time face to face.

I looked into her eyes as I took her slow and deep.

"I own you Arianna Rossi; you'll never escape me now." Her eyes glazed over.

I lifted her legs high up on my back and ground myself into her making her cry out.

"My little mob girl likes to fuck." Her hips were grinding against mine.

I kissed her before she could respond.

The first time had been a mating, a taming if you will, this time was so she knew there will be gentleness as well, though I was sure there would be some serious fucking going on.

We fucked each other until we were both exhausted, I had to ice her pussy because she complained, and no, she still didn't get to be on top. It was going to take a while for me to master her, for now I would do the fucking. When she learned to mind me then I'll think of giving her the reins.

I'm sure she'd have my dick if she knew what I was thinking but what the hell. A man had to rule his home after all.

I think I stood a better chance against my enemies than against mouth though.

Join me next time for more of Shane and his Mouth in Lady Boss.

It's morning' for some stupid fuck reason I got up with the need to take her out to breakfast. I just had the urge to see her sitting across a table from me in a crowded place while we enjoyed something as simple as breakfast, normal right? Forgot I was talking about Mouth.

First she moaned and groaned about being awakened too early in the morning for sex.

"Listen Lancelot, my coochie goes on lock down until at least nine in the damn A.M, no overtime, write a memo, memorize that shit."

"Do you ever stop?"

"Is this or is it not my coochie?"

"It's mine now."

I had to wrestle with her ass to open her legs; I ended up holding both her hands in one of mine while prying her legs open with the other. Crazy lady was trying to bite me.

I pushed two fingers deep inside her to calm her ass down.

Lady Boss

by

Jordan Silver

Table of Contents

Chapter 1

It's morning and for some stupid fuck reason I got up with the need to take her out to breakfast; I just had the urge to see her sitting across a table from me in a crowded place while we enjoyed something as a simple as breakfast, normal right? Forgot I was talking about Mouth.

First she moaned and groaned about being awakened too early in the morning for sex.

"Listen Lancelot, my coochie goes on lock down until at least nine in the damn A.M, no overtime write a memo, and memorize that shit."

"Do you ever stop?"

"Is this or is it not my coochie?"

"It's mine now."

I had to wrestle with her ass to open her legs; I ended up holding both her hands in one of mine while prying her legs open with the other. Crazy lady was trying to bite me.

I pushed two fingers deep inside her to calm her ass down.

"Ummmmm, okay, if you can keep that up you can get you some, but don't make it a habit."

"Open your legs and close your mouth."

"Uh huh." She gave me shit but did it anyway.

I worked her over with my fingers, then my mouth because I couldn't resist the taste of her.

It seems she became a completely different person when I put my hands on her. All that fire in her tongue went straight to her pussy. She was sweet and wild and it drove me fucking crazy.

If I wasn't careful she would soon be leading me around by my fucking dick.

"Dammit." That's all I heard before she flooded my mouth, she pulled my hair so tight I wasn't sure if she was pulling me closer or trying to push me away. Whatever! I wasn't finished eating her.

I kept my tongue inside her while I teased her clit with my fingers.

"It's too much Shane."

Her body was shaking as her nectar flowed onto my tongue.

"Take it babe." I gave her a few more licks, nipped her clit, and then climbed up her body burying my cock to the root.

I wasn't going to last too long, which seemed to be my usual plight where she was concerned.

"Fuck Ari why is your pussy so fucking good, damn?"

She was squeezing and pulling on me like nothing I've ever felt before.

"Give me your mouth."

She licked and bit my bottom lip before sucking my tongue into the vortex of her mouth.

Now her eyes were doing that dreamy look thing they did whenever I fucked her, like the pleasure was too much and she was drifting on another plane.

"Harder Shane..."

"Get up."

I pulled her up, her legs went around my hips, and mine were under her in a sitting position.

This way I could look into her eyes as we moved together, it also drove me deeper into her core, which made her arch her back, thrusting her beautiful tits in my face.

"Hmmm." I tasted her soft flesh with my tongue.

"I can't wait to give you my son."

Ah, you liked that did you? Your mouth might say one thing but your body can't lie. She'd clenched around me at my words.

I looked at her, really looked at her, in this position it was hard not to.

My heart clenched. Fuck, fuck me, how did she do it?

I didn't even realize I had stopped moving until she gave me this quizzical look and tried to get me to move.

"What...?"

I could only shake my head as I started to move again. How could I tell her that in her eyes I saw forever? What kinda sappy ass fuckery was this; I was fucking falling for this girl.

I reared up forcing her back onto the bed; her legs were caught high up on my back giving me more room to plow into her at will.

I needed to pound out whatever the fuck this was that was clawing its way up my throat.

"Fuck, shit, damn."

She was going through her repertoire of swear words I guess as I thrust harder and faster, it was a race against the turmoil going on inside me. When I came I went blind, deaf, and dumb.

She'd sucked my essence from me that time.

Now we're dressed and ready to go. She's wearing one of my dress shirts tied at the waist with a pair of low rider jeans, she looks hot as fuck with her hair wild and all over the place.

Her lips were red and swollen and she looked freshly fucked. I'd left a nice little hickey on the side of her throat; I don't think she noticed it yet. There will probably be hell to pay when she did.

"Are they likely to be any of your friendly neighbors shooting at us this morning John Gotti?"

She never stopped, and what the fuck was her fascination with the mob?

"What's with you and the godfathers Mouth, you study this shit or what?"

"I just find the criminal mind so compelling, not to mention batshit crazy."

"Who you calling crazy?" I put her in a playful headlock.

"If the cement shoe fits...."

"Let's go eat."

"Don't you need to call Fredo and Carmine?"

"My guys are already here."

"You never answered my question, will there be any disgruntled Capo de capos shooting us up, I don't think I can run in these shoes."

She looked down at the stilts she had on her feet, fucking women.

"Nothing for you to worry about, ever, that's my shit to deal with not yours."

"Just so you know those imaginary sons of yours if they ever do exist are going to etiquette school."

"You're not turning my sons into pussies."

"Open the door douche bag."

"I'm getting on it, give me a sec."

I pulled out my phone to check in with my detail and hers, just because she was with me didn't mean she didn't still have Tommy on her ass, of course I had to talk in code so she wouldn't understand what I was saying to him.

I hung up the phone and opened the door for the mouthy one.

"That that dark haired guy that's been following me for about a week?"

"What the fuck?"

Chapter 2

Prince of the City

How the fuck had she made Tommy? Had he been carless or was she just that observant? I had to play this shit off or who knows what the fuck would come of it.

"Who's following you crazy lady?"

"The guy you were just talking to, I hope he doesn't sit in that car all day while I'm in class, you might as well pay me the money to look out for myself.

"Whatever, we'll deal with your paranoia later; right now I just want to take my woman out to breakfast."

"Uh huh, paranoid my ass, you tell Tessio if he's going to be tailing me he might as well give me a ride, I could save on gas, it would be good for the environment."

"Would you quit it, damn; can we just go have breakfast like normal people?"

"Listen John Roselli, only one of us is normal and it ain't you."

"Plan on dumping me in a steel drum do ya?"

"Don't forget the sawed off legs part, handsome Johnny."

She had the nerve to laugh in my face, I didn't know what my life was gonna be like, half the time I didn't know whether to fuck her or strangle her.

As I walked her through the door being sure to keep her on my inside away from harm, my phone rang.

Mom calling.

"Ma?"

"Good morning son, how are you this fine morning?"

Oh shit, she was up to something, whenever she got this sugary sweet it always meant my ass was on the line for something.

"I'm good, I'm about to take Arianna to breakfast."

"Oh how sweet, actually that's why I'm calling, I want Ari here for Sunday dinner, if the girl is going to be part of the family we might as well throw her into the deep end of the pool right off, don't you think so sweetheart?"

Well fuck me, I knew she would eventually have to come but not this soon, not only was I not ready to share her with anybody, not even my own mother, but too much exposure to the females in my family was not a food thing.

"Uhhh......"

"That's wonderful son, so we'll see you at your usual time, and could you please do something with your brother, he's gone strange all of a sudden."

Oh fuck I forgot all about Mouth and Jimmy, how the hell can I get out of this shit? If I missed Sunday dinner ma would have a fit of astronomical proportions, I couldn't leave Mouth alone not with the Staccos still on the loose. They'd gone into hiding and it was taking me a minute to flush them out, not that I was worried, I wasn't the best in the business because of my looks, I got shit done when it needed doing.

Now instead of doing my shit I have to deal with the women in my life, give me the Staccos and their fuckery please. I didn't mouth off to ma, just made noises in her ear that she wanted to hear and hung up the phone.

"Afraid of your mother are you?"

We had reached the car and of course those two fucks overheard her and started laughing, when did I lose my edge, when did people start disrespecting my manhood?

I gave the two of them a glare, seated her next to me in the back with my hand thrown over her shoulders and kept my mouth shut. It was too early in the damn day for this shit.

Breakfast was interesting as was to be expected, Mouth thought she was eating toast and coffee, I had other ideas, you can imagine how that went.

"You need to eat, that's not enough food to feed a cat, bring her the steak and eggs, hash browns, and toast, you want pancakes Mouth......?"

She was busy ignoring me; the poor waitress looked like she would rather be in Outer Mongolia right about now.

"Oh, you finish trying to feed the free world, I can order now? Thank you, as I was saying ...what's your name, uh, Sandy, as I was saying, wheat toast with butter and coffee black."

"Mouth swear to God, I will force feed you this shit, you're not going all day on toast and coffee, not on my watch, bring what I ordered please."

Good at least the waitress still feared me, somebody around here was acting like they had some sense, the peanut gallery was fighting their laughter, elbowing each other on the sly.

What happened to the hard asses that I've known all my life, she'd turned all of us into pansy asses. My glares were barely working these days.

The food came and as you can imagine there was a standoff, I meant to win this war though , I never understood why women starved themselves like that, I would never have expected it of Mouth though, she just didn't seem the type, besides I'd seen her throwing down in my kitchen so that couldn't be it, and why in the hell did she keep looking around, she's doing it in a very circumspect way but I was attuned to her, it was almost as though she was casing the joint, what the fuck?

"Eat Arianna, I got you covered."

"What, what do you mean?"

"It just occurred to me that although you didn't make a big deal out of being shot at it must still be a bit of a shock, and maybe you're expecting some shit to go down again whenever you're with me, I'm just letting you know that I have you covered, my guys are on the job so there's no need for you to worry."

She fidgeted for a second, tried to pull it back in but I had seen her unease.

"I'm fine, really, no worries."

Uh huh that's why you just picked up your fork and started eating the food you just told me you refuse to eat. Yep she was scared that something would go down, I couldn't have that, if I wanted to take my woman out to eat she was supposed to be happy, relaxed, not looking around corners for the fucking boogeyman, the Staccos were so fucked.

She talked me into letting her go to her place for some clothes after breakfast; since I wasn't born yesterday I went with her, we argued the whole way there.

"Arianna just open the damn door so we can get this over with. I pushed her inside when she opened the door.

Two things registered as soon as we entered, one I could smell men's cologne, and two there was someone here.

I pushed her behind me just as I registered the older man with the gun. The fuck. I could draw and shoot in a second if needed but what if he hit her.

What the fuck Shane, you're slipping.

As I pulled my gun out and aimed Mouth came around beside me.

"Uncle Alphonso put that gun away, this one's mine."

"He's what?"

"Mine, you know my one and only true love, all that bullshit you and dad used to feed me when I was little."

"Principessa." He smiled wide and opened his arms.

"What the fuck did you just call her?"

Chapter 3

"Ari Mia who is this yahoo?"

"She isn't your anything old man, watch what the fuck you call my woman in front of me."

Shane stepped towards him as if he was about to throw down.

I placed myself between them, men were so pig headed, "Cool it Michael Corleone, no one's taking out the five families today."

"You still doing that shit Ari MIA?" Shane pointed his gun at him again and I gave my uncle a glare, he was just provoking Shane on purpose now.

"Put that thing down, it's fine I promise." He lowered his gun but kept his eyes on uncle Alphonso.

"What shit?" He finally asked.

"Quoting mobster flicks, how many files you got now by the way Principessa?"

"All of them." I smirked at him; I'd pulled off something none of the others could in all the years they'd been trying. I had the files of every sitting head in America.

"Damn, you are selling?"

"I ain't no stinking snitch."

"Whatever, what are you doing in this dump?"

"This is a dump?" Shane looked confused.

"Compared to her home it is."

"Uncle Al, ssshh."

"Oh no you don't Mouth, start talking."

Oh shit, I wrung my hands together going for my innocent look, how to tell him, he's going to flip, I looked to uncle Alphonso.

"You told me to sshh remember."

I rolled my eyes at him, now he decides to listen to me, old blabber mouth; I wondered what game he was playing now.

"MyfatheristheheadoftheChicagofamilies."

"Your what?"

"Her father is Roberto Rossi, maybe you've heard of him in this bumfuck town."

"The fuck?" He looked dazed, yeah; my dad had been the baddest of the bad.

"Speaking of which Ari, I might have a surprise for you."

"Ooh, I almost forgot, what did you bring me?"

He inclined his head to the gift bag on the table. I ran over squealing like a school girl.

"Are you two bent, Arianna get over here."

"Keep your shorts on there little Nicky." I took the snow globe from its silk wrapping paper. "Ooh wait, I have this one."

"No you don't."

"I think I do."

"No you don't, your dad and I have a scrap book of all the ones you have and that's not in it."

"We'll see."

"About that surprise....."

"This wasn't it?"

"If you two are finished with family hour there's a little matter I would like to discuss, like how the fuck my wife ends up being the daughter of one of the most notorious mob bosses to grace our great nation?"

"You got married without us?" Uncle Al looked hurt.

"No uncle, Shane here prides himself on being a forward thinker; he thinks he only has to say something to make it so."

"So you're not marrying him?"

"Yes the fuck she is, or I don't care who her father used to be, I will fuck everybody's shit up, now one of you start talking, preferably you Mouth, did you play me?"

"What, of course not, why the hell would I do that?"

"I don't know, why didn't you tell me who you are?"

"What's it to ya?"

"Mouth, swear to God."

"Look, I don't have anything to do with that cops and robbers game you grown men like to play, I came here to get away from all that; I found some notes in day's office about this place and thought it was as good a place as any." I kept my fingers crossed where they couldn't see; lying is such a shit fuck thing to do. Damn I'm starting to sound like Shane.

"So how did you find me Uncle Al?"

"It wasn't easy let me tell you, I wasn't expecting to find you hooked up with the local head, seeing as how you're so averse to the family business and all." He had that gleam in his eye. He's been trying my whole life to turn me into a boy.

"Don't even think about it, I'm not taking over that mess....."

"What the fuck Mouth, you're the heir to the Chicago Cartel?"

"Nope....."

"Speaking of which Ari Mia, about that surprise......"

"Hello baby girl."

I spun around so fast I almost gave myself whiplash. No it couldn't be.

"Dad?"

"In the flesh baby girl." He opened his arms for a hug, big sappy grin on his face.

"Shane give me your gun."

"Now Arianna calm down, you don't want to shoot your old man again do you?"

"Again?" Poor Shane was trying to keep up.

"When I was three he left his gun on the table, I mistakenly shot him....... in the ass."

The jerk started howling with laughter.

"Whatever, dad, what the hell?"

"Sorry." He gave me a sheepish look.

"Sorry, sorry, you let me think you were dead all this time...?"

"It wasn't that long bambina, besides I couldn't tell you what was going on, it had to look legit, if you knew I was alive then you wouldn't have grieved the right way and our enemies would've known something was up. By the way that was a nice turn out I had, you did me proud ......"

"You were there?" I was back to trying to find a gun, this was too much even for him.

"That fuck Louis lump lump wasn't there though, friend my ass."

"Dad you called him Louis lump lump his whole life even when you were kids, why would he come to your funeral?"

"To show his respect fat fuck, I got something for him though."

"You leave Uncle Louis alone; he wasn't there because he was doing something for me."

"What, computer shit, cause that's all that fat fuck is any good for."

"Yes, he was gathering information so I could find out who put the hit out on you."

"Which led you here, which is only one more reason why I should put a hole in his fat ass."

"Boy you Rossis sure like shooting people in the ass."

I gave Shane the bitch brow to no avail; let him laugh now, in about five minutes he was going to be back to being pissed.

"Anyway, since no one killed you my work here is done."

"You know little girl, for someone who always swore she didn't want anything to do with family business you sure do think like a boss."

"Stow it dad, I was just going to do this one job."

"My girl was going to avenge her old man, see Alphonso, I told you she was just like her dad."

"As I recall you bitched at me for turning your daughter into my nephew, now you wanna reap the benefits. I think she's got a little bit of both if us. Pure gangster."

"You wish, now what the hell is going on?"

"First, what the hell is going on with you and Flanagan, you ride me your whole life about my doings only to end up with my double?"

Chapter 4

Prince of the City

I'm trying to take all this shit in, I had a mafia princess in my jurisdiction for a while and had no idea, how the fuck did she slip by my guys, she wasn't even using an alias, not that anyone knew too much about Rossi's only offspring, she was one of the mob's best kept secrets.

"Swear to me that you didn't play me Mouth."

I could forgive anything but the thought that she might've played me wasn't one of them, I'd let her into my circle, introduced her to ma; fuck, ma.

"I didn't even know who you were, my research was only concentrated on the ones who took out dad, believe me I only found out about you after I got here, and since you weren't on my hit list I had no real interest in you."

"Wait, your hit list, what the fuck, you're not hitting anybody, what the hell would I tell our kids?"

"Uhhh, what do you plan on telling them about you?"

"I'm a man; my boys will expect me to handle shit."

"First of all, our daughters aren't going to be anywhere near this mess....."

"When's the wedding?"

That Alphonso prick piped in, I wasn't sure about him, he seems to like egging her on, encouraging her in shit. Her father had been a little tongue in cheek when he'd made that crack about her not wanting anything to do with the business too.

"Wait, what wedding, nobody asked me about this."

"Dad you're dead, and I'm eighteen nobody needs your permission to do anything."

"That's what you think, do you have any idea what the ciuccio that marries you stand to inherit, he'll become my heir."

"No he wouldn't, stop it dad..."

"Of course he would, since you refuse the position, which is a pain in my heart, but he would become heir in your stead; but bambina, this medigan?"

"Roberto, how many times must I tell you, come out of the dark ages brother, besides you know la Principessa never does the expected?"

"Yeah Al but....."

"Can we get back to the matter at hand, and I'll ignore the insults Rossi, just don't make it a habit."

Badass or not, no one was going to disrespect me on my turf, future father in law or not.

"What matter would that be young blood?"

"The matter of why my future wife was here in the first place, someone in my territory put a hit out on you?"

"Yeah, you could say that, but it goes deeper than that, it was a takeover attempt that was supposed to cover the whole of the Western faction."

"What do you mean take over the whole of the west, that would include me and that shit's not about to happen, what's going on?"

"Well it's like this, you have a family here that's associated with a family in my back yard, these two fucks got together and cooked up a scheme of how to take over, they were going to hit me first and then after a little time had gone by and the heat died down they were coming for you and all the other heads, but since you and I are the strongest opposition we were first."

"Yeah but my dealings don't mesh with yours and your territory ends a state over from here, so how did I get involved?"

"Didn't I just say they want the whole of the West?"

"And how does Mouth play into this, if she is your heir....."

"She was supposed to be forced to marry Carlo Stacco."

"The fuck you say?"

Chapter 5

Prince of the City

"You're not fucking marrying Carlo Stacco. The fuck?" She rolled her eyes at me before giving me the 'you're stupid' look. I walked to where she was standing and dragged her into my side.

The two murdering old fucks got a chuckle out of that.

"I didn't say she was going to marry the prick, I said that's what they were going to try. Get her to marry him so he could lead through her or at least that's what the organization was supposed to believe. Like we're fucking dopes, but our girl flew the coop before they could put that shit in motion.

Which brings me back to my question, what're you doing in this dump?"

"My place isn't a fucking dump, what I want to know is how the fuck did you get in here?"

"Son that's my specialty. Getting in and out of places."

I gave Mouth a squeeze; I guess that answered the question of how she got out of my bedroom.

When he grinned at her, I knew I'd been right, the fuck had taught her all he knew most likely. If I caught her doing any more of that mob shit I was gonna kick her ass. My wife was supposed to be a stay at home mom who baked fucking cookies and shit, just like ma, not running around the place picking locks. Fuck my life, why me?

"My guards downstairs didn't see you two come in, I wanna know how you got into my place without being noticed."

"Can't share trade secrets son, not until you're part of the family anyways." Her jerk of an uncle was really beginning to work my fucking nerves.

"Is anyone going to tell me what the fuck's going on here, I don't like too many of you on my turf, I get kinda twitchy when other bosses stay too long in my backyard, especially without my invite."

Boss of bosses or not, no one was going to disrespect me, then again he was my new father in law so I could be a little more lenient, somebody's head was gonna roll though cause there's no way they breeched my security, I'm not that fucking green.

"I'm here for my daughter; if her uncle was watching her like he was supposed to we wouldn't be here.

"Don't start Roberto, you taught the brat how to evade and disappear, I had a hell of a time finding her, that fat fuck held out on me even when I threatened to off his mother, and then we got lucky." He smiled at me like he knew something I didn't. What the fuck?

"Uncle Al you didn't."

"Sure did brat, I would've offed the old bag too if I had to; now what the hell are you doing in Flanagan's bed, didn't we teach you any better than that?"

"Hey, watch your fucking mouth, the fuck's that supposed to mean?"

"Keep your shorts on young blood, all I meant was that if she's trying to get out of the life then she shouldn't be shacking up with you."

"Yeah Ari, my feelings are hurt, you tormented your poor old man for years about this life and now you're hooked up with mini me." Her father gave her a sulky look, some mafia boss he was.

I know one thing, if these fuck didn't stop insulting me I was gonna pop a cap in somebody's ass, preferably the uncle's. I still didn't like him being all cozy with my girl, but that was for later. Right now I had more important things to deal with.

"What's going on with you and the Staccos?"

I faced the two of them, arms folded, face stern so they knew I meant business, I may be younger than they are, but this was still my territory and they had broken into my place, we all knew the only reason they were still breathing was because of my woman.

"I told you already, they put a hit out on me."

"Yeah but where does things stand now, how're you handling this shit and how the fuck do we get Mouth out of the middle of this fuckery?"

"Mouth, that's what you call her, that's perfect."

"Dad zip it."

"See, always was a mouthy little thing you sure you can handle her Flanagan, of course I have yet to give my blessing, we're gonna have to have a sit down when this is all over."

"I hear what you're saying she's your daughter, but understand when I took her to my bed I didn't know that, now it makes no difference to me, she's mine."

"Shane,....I can't believe you just told my dad that we went to bed together, what are you new?" She put her face in her palm and shook her head.

Before I could answer her there was a crashing sound and Michael and Anthony bounded through the door, guns drawn.

Pretty soon there were six guns pointing in two directions.

"Mouth, where the fuck did you get that gun? Put that thing away."

Okay, I knew about the shooting incident with my little brother the fuck, but seeing how smoothly she drew her weapon, the familiar ease with which she held it, didn't sit too well with me. My wife shouldn't be handling guns. Fuck no.

"The fuck Shane, we've been calling you for ten minutes."

Shit, I forgot all about them.

"Put the guns away boys, we've got company."

"Fuck.....you're Roberto Rossi...and you're Alphonso Rossi......" Trust Tony to know who they were, he was almost as bad as Mouth with the mob trivia.

"Wait a minute, Arianna...you're Arianna fucking Rossi Mouth? Oh shit, she's like royalty." Mikey was having an Oprah moment or some shit. "Wait 'til I tell ma about this."

Oh fuck.

"Nobody's telling ma about anything, now if you two girls would like to come in and close the door we've got some shit to deal with, it seems Stacco is after Arianna as well."

"What the fuck for?" Mikey bristled.

"Can I finish ...apparently the Staccos and some other faction from Rossi's territory has decided to combine their efforts to overthrow not only Rossi's organization, but ours as well, they want to head the west coast families together.

In order to do that they need to get rid of both of us. They think they've already taken out the old man, so I'm the only thing standing in their way, except to take over Rossi's side of things they need his only heir, which would be Mouth.

The plan is for Carlo Stacco to force her into marriage against her will if necessary, take over, and run things in her name. So now things have escalated, I want to know where that fuck is yesterday, it's just become personal."

"What the fuck was it before Shane?"

"Business Mikey, now my woman's involved, I'm gonna cap that bitch ass motherfucker right after I cut his fucking dick off."

Mouth who had been unusually quiet throughout my tirade rolled her eyes at me. I scowled at her in an obvious message of keep out of it, but did crazy mob girl listen, of course not.

"Take it easy there Joe Bonano, don't go off half cocked...."

"Mouth."

"No hear me out, I've been working this for months, ever since they hit my dad." She gave him a scathing look.

"You're not involved, give me what you've got, but you're out of it, from now on you don't do anything you hear me?"

"Uh, are you off your meds again ...bless your heart? You don't get to tell me what to do capisce?"

I was back to wanting to pop her one, I should be able to get away with it for all the aggravation she's caused me.

"Mouth, I'll fucking lock you away somewhere, swear on my mother."

"Let me know how you make out with that one........jackass."

I pulled her in and bit into her bottom lip just to shut her up, but I'd overplayed my hand. I'd forgotten how the taste of her went straight to my head, and how she always just stopped whenever I touched her. It was like pulling a switch; she melted into me with a sigh. I took her mouth forgetting our audience until I heard throat clearing and chuckles.

"Boy you're mighty brave manhandling my kid in front of me like that; I guess any man who has the coglioni to do that is good enough to be my son in law, my male heir." He actually rubbed his hands together.

"Even though you're medigan, I would've chosen a nice Italian boy for you though Ari, but when have you ever listened to me?"

I was ready to go apeshit when he mentioned choosing an Italian as her mate but Mouth calmed the situation.

"Dad you knew there wasn't a snowball's chance in hell that I'd ever marry one of your cronies or any of their deadbeat sons, knock it off."

"See Roberto that's gratitude for ya, I told you we shoulda sent her to the nuns when she was little, she's got way too much fire in her, that can't be good."

"She gets it from her mother, God rest her soul."

"You're right about that, Dahlia was known to have a temper." He laughed in fond remembrance.

"Are we through with family hour, because I heard something about some asshole plotting to take me out so he can take over my shit, not only that now I have to deal with the fact that said asshole's son was planning to kidnap and force my wife into marriage."

"Uh..." Mouth raised her hand as if to interrupt, but since I knew what she was about to say I cut her off at the pass. She's my wife in my eyes and that's fucking final.

"You're as good as; I don't need to hear it from you. Now what the fuck are we going to do about these fucks?" I turned back to her annoying family.

"What you got Ari?" Rossi looked at his daughter expectantly, it didn't escape my notice that he still hadn't gotten too close to Mouth, he must really think she would slug him for making her believe he was dead all this time.

She folded her arms and tapped her foot, aw shit, here comes the fucking attitude. Fuck my life, will she ever just do as she's told, I guess not, hard headed fuck. She's going to make me batty. This is what I'd chosen for myself, this is what I took one look at and decided I had to have it. Fuck me.

"I want in, I did all the ground work it's only fair." I opened my mouth to blast her, no fucking way, if she thought I was kidding she could think again, I don't care what she'd gotten up to before she became mine, but there was no way I was standing back and letting her put herself in harm's way ever again though. Ma would have a coronary if she heard about this shit. She liked to pretend that I was just a night club owner; I liked to keep it that way.

"Be reasonable Arianna, you never wanted any part of the life remember and this thing is big, this could mean all out war. Flanagan's right, you need to stay out of this."

"Dead man talking. No." She actually held her palm up to him.

Damn she even gives Roberto Rossi shit, this did not bode well for me, she was gonna run circles around my ass for sure. Shit, I am so fucked.

Right now I have to find a diplomatic way to get her to pull out, she had that mutinous look on her face which meant we would be here all night with the back and forth and I wanted to get things rolling as soon as possible. Somehow knowing they were after her was more significant than them wanting me dead, and that's just plain fucked up. I think I might've borrowed Mikey's vagina. Pussy whipped motherfucker.

"Okay Mouth, you got a point, you did the ground work, let’s see what you've got and we'll go from there."

"Uh uh, promise me first and then I'll share."

I had to give my wording some thought, couldn't lie to my woman now could I, that's no way to start a relationship, not to mention crazy woman would have my nuts if I fucked with her.

"Okay, I promise that we'll let you help with the situation."

"Thank you." She smiled and headed towards her bedroom returning with a box full of folders and what looked like her school shit.

"Fuck Mouth, how long you been on these guys?" She preened at me so I stole a smooch.

"Alright you two knock it off, Flanagan I hope you know what you're doing letting her get involved, she's obviously not listening to anything I say, not that she ever did. I can make grown men shit themselves but this little bit of a thing ignores me, now how fair is that I ask you?"

"Karma dad, suck it up and stop whining."

She spread her notes and shit all over the dinner table. She had dates, photos, transcribed conversations from wiretapping; I don't even want to know how she got that shit.

She knew hiding places, hangouts, where the mistresses were kept. The shit was like an organized sting by a one woman force. Who the fuck was this girl?

"Mouth when you have time to do all this, weren't you in school?"

The peanut gallery found that funny, I glowered at the two old fucks, but they kept laughing. I get no fucking respect anymore.

"Uhm, about that, I take one class in the mornings, but the rest of the day I do recon." She bit her thumb nail, I got suspicious.

"And then what, you go back to school in the evenings so Tommy can follow you home?"

"About that young blood..." Her uncle Alphonso cleared his throat, how did I know that I wasn't going to like what came out of his mouth next.

"Tommy's ours..."

"He's what?"

"We sent him to you, when we learned about the hit on Roberto and the takeover here, we didn't know too much about you at the time so we thought to play it safe and get a man on the inside."

"You know him? So that shit you gave me earlier about him following you?" I had Mouth by the shoulders.

"I didn't know he was here until you had him tailing me." She held up her hands.

"So why did you still give me shit, you knew by then...."

"Just my way of messing with you....." Cocky grin, I pulled my hair, what the fuck, I felt like I was spinning out of control, how had all these things happened without me knowing, I obviously had to go through my organization for any more moles. Most of the guys were from grandpa's time, if not his men then their sons and nephews. That's how it was; the mob is an incestuous bitch.

I turned to Mikey and Tony. "When this shit is done I'm calling a meeting, I don't want any more surprises, the fucking Chicago mafia infiltrated us, and we had no fucking clue, who else did?"

"You're clean Flanagan, we did a run on all your men, not only did your grandfather run a tight ship, but you've got a good head on your shoulders. You were looking for the best and you got it, Tommy is the best at what he does, the fact that you put him on my daughter goes a long way to proving to me where she stands with you. Trust me if these things weren't adding up in your favor there's no way she would be marrying you?"

"Wanna bet?" I'd shoot his ass right here......

"Take it easy Tommy two thumbs don't shoot the cadaver, we've got things to do." She pushed me towards the table.

Chapter 6

Prince of the City

We went back to reading and planning. I called out for food around seven in the evening we'd been poring over her notes for hours.

I had her sitting next to me so I could feel her, know she was safe, because each time I read how she had broken into some place or the other my blood ran cold.

The fact that she'd been in danger all this time, in my own backyard made me see red. When I got to the part about someone breaking into her bedroom back at home in Chicago I wanted to tear the motherfucker apart.

Luckily she'd been out gathering information that night and had escaped whatever the fuck had been in store for her. She'd left the next day, no wonder.

Now we knew the Staccos had tried to make good on their kidnapping threat. Dead motherfuckers, they were getting more and more dead by the minute.

I pulled out my phone at the end of my rope, fuck this shit.

"Where the fuck is Stacco?" I listened to the voice on the other end of the line. My men knew better than to make any excuses to me, especially when I used that tone of voice.

I hung up after getting the information, not what I wanted but it'll do for now.

"Let's roll." I was talking to Mikey and Tony but the other three got up as well.

"Fuck you two coming with?" Who the fuck was supposed to lead in this situation, I don't brush up on mobster one o one like these Chicago freaks, they probably had some kind of etiquette attached to this shit, well I never had any intentions on going on a hit with another boss, the fuck do I know about this shit?

It's my turf, but this guy outranks me in our world, sorta, know what I mean, not to mention he's my new father in law on top of that, they'd tried to hit him, he deserved retribution, fuck.

They were checking their guns; including my little gentle violet. Breathe the sarcasm.

"Mouth you're not going."

"What...you promised."

"Yes I did and I will keep my promise that you can help us in this situation, you can be of great help by trying to decode those cryptic messages you intercepted."

"Nice try Carmine Persico, but no dice, a deals a deal welch."

"Fuck." I had my head down, my hand to my forehead as if thinking really hard. Know your enemy. The Art of War one o one, she read that shit too though, she'd be watching for my play, my baby was smart. Gotta be smarter, how was I gonna play this?

There's no way in hell she's going, fuck that. Ma would have my balls for sure I take her new daughter in law out on a hit, uhuh.

"Okay, but if we're gonna do this then you have to wear a vest.......I don't want to hear it." I cut her off as soon as she opened her mouth to argue.

"If you want to come along you have to wear one."

"Where am I supposed to get a vest?" Now we were in a face off.

"What am I an amateur, let's go."

She gave me a suspicious look before following me to the door.

"I don't know about this new son in law of mine Alphonso, he doesn't seem to be any better at handling her than I am."

I ignored the old man as I led her to my place. Mutt and Jeff were behind us with shit eating grins on their faces. Assholes, I gave them each a glare which did nothing to stop their disrespectful behavior. No doubt ma and the girls will be getting a play by play first chance they get. Gossiping fucks.

Unlocking the door I walked ahead of Ari as the boys who were now joined by the two old gangsters waited in the living room.

I walked into my walk in closet and touched the crease that hid the mechanism that opened my weapons slash safe room.

I walked in so she would see I wasn't up to anything. Grabbing the new ultra thin bodysuit that's really a bulletproof vest in disguise, I passed it off to her.

When she reached to take it I cuffed her left hand, pulled it behind her back, and attached it to her right.

"You asshole jerk." She rammed her head back into my chest.

"Oomph, stop it Mouth, you know you don't have any right being in on a hit, you know I can't do it, I can't take you into danger baby please...just stay here I'll make it quick."

She turned her head away from me. "Mouth, Mouth look at me." I had to turn her head to me, she looked ready to kill, but she didn't say a word. I gave her a quick kiss not trying for anything longer since I needed my tongue for the duration of my existence on this earth and I was quite sure she'd do her damnedest to chew it off it I tried.

"It's going to be okay." I brushed her hair back and kissed her forehead. She pulled away from me.

Fuck me, and so it begins. The last thing I saw before closing the reinforced steel door was the look of betrayal in her eyes. Now I felt like shit.

"Let's move, I'll give you guys the Intel on the way there." I talked as I walked.

"Where's Ari?" Rossi looked behind me as though expecting to see her there.

"Don't ask she's safe."

"Oh shit son, you sure you wanna do this?"

"Yes Alphonso, what do you suggest, should I take my wife on a hit, would you take yours?"

"Well now, I don't have a wife and the one you're planning to marry isn't exactly the norm if you know what I mean. Arianna is........well, let's just say she's not going to take this lightly."

"Tell me something I don't know, at least this way I don't have to worry about her little ass being hurt. Now are we going or do you have more marital advice to share?"

"Come on Al, Flanagan's got it all figured out, don't say we didn't warn you boy, my little girl isn't known for her forgiving nature, shit like this could play out for months."

"Yeah Roberto, remember her senior prom, that finocchio she wanted to go with.....?" They went out the door reminiscing about Mouth and her penchant for retaliation and holding a grudge.

I gave one last look in the direction of my bedroom, my heart heavy. I know she felt betrayed but I'd rather have her pissed the fuck off than dead.

She'd just have to get over it, and I'll just have to love her out of her funk. See no one before me had that weapon in their arsenal. I could use my charms on her, give her some good loving and all's forgiven. Yeah if she doesn't castrate my ass first. Ouch.

I had to put that shit away for now; I had an asshole to burn.

Chapter 7

Prince of the City

I'd decided, my turf, my woman, my hit.

My guest will just have to take a back seat, it's not like I could move into their territory and make a hit. Besides I owed the Staccos, they'd been fucking with me for way too long.

The son was still hiding somewhere but I had a bead on the father, one's good enough for now. I had no doubt that if I hit the father the son would come out of hiding.

Him I wanted to spend some time with, marry my girl indeed. The fuck, what he'd planned amounted to rape. He was going to force my Ari, like fuck. I'm gonna enjoy fucking him up.

"Carmine Stacco is holed up in a cabin in the forest two hours outside of town, no word yet on where his spawn is but I'm sure when news of his father's demise reaches him we'll flush him out."

I imparted that info while we rode down in the elevator, everyone had their game face on now; everything else was forgotten as my detail fell in behind me when we reached the ground floor.

My guards didn't seem surprised to see the two new additions and I understood when Tommy showed his face.

I gave him a look that said I didn't appreciate the bullshit even if he was there to protect me, I should've been told from the get what the fuck was going on. He fell in with the others as we headed to the garage. I'll deal with that shit later; right now I was fighting to keep my mind off the she devil I'd just locked in a safe room. My balls curled up at the mere thought of what hell she was gonna unleash on my ass.

I put all thoughts other than what I was about to face out of my head, you never went into a situation without a clear head.

There wasn't much to it anyhow, they already knew what they needed to know about the set up, what Stacco and his counterpart had had planned, after this I would have to sit down with them and get names and shit because there's no way they thought they could bring us down without inside help, which meant most likely that someone in my organization was a sellout. Another dead mother fucker.

No one said much of anything in the car, this was serious business, we were about to end a man, that shit was not to be taken lightly, the only thing I killed without mercy was a roach.

The cabin was hidden in the dense woods, there was very little light inside or out, and my Intel had three men here with him on guard.

Mikey and Tony got down to business using heat seeking equipment to find the bodies.

We had parked away from the place and walked in on a spread out. I only had Tony, Mikey and the Rossis with me, my other boys were back up and lookouts, I didn't need a whole platoon to take out one old man and three guards, usually for a hit like this it would just be the three of us but these two wanted in, I was even tempted to let Rossi take him and save mine for the son, but this fuck had caused me to trap my girl in a room and I know she was gonna be pissed as fuck, so I should at least get to kick his ass.

So much for putting that shit away, even here she was never far from my mind.

There were three bodies spread out in one room in the cabin and a solo form lying prone on a bed in one of the bedrooms.

The blueprints had shown that there were four bedrooms, Stacco was in the third from the front, there was a window there which had been discretely left unlatched for us, we could go in, do him, and walk away, the guards would never know, but if we wanted to fuck him over first we'd need to off them first.

"You want him?"

"Fuck yeah boy."

"Window." I stepped back, my sign that he should take the lead.

"You leaving the guards?"

"They didn't do anything to me; they're just doing their jobs that are not how I roll."

Rossi turned and looked at Alphonso, then he smiled slowly, nodded, and walked ahead.

I spent ten seconds wondering what that whole exchange was about before putting my head on straight and following him.

Tony, Mikey, and I stood watch keeping an eye on the bodies in the living room watching TV while the two old mobsters went around the other side. We could watch them as well so if anything went awry we could step in.

We saw them pull the window up and had a tense moment when the body on the bed moved. Okay, he was just turning over.

Rossi stood over him with a hand over his mouth and a gun to his temple, I wish I could hear what he was saying to the other man, maybe I'll ask him later.

We saw the recoil from the gun, the head drop back to the bed and the two men leaving out through the window. The guards never moved from their places. Silencers were the shit.

Chapter 8

Back in the car the tension was gone, everyone seemed relaxed, and of course the conversation turned to my upcoming demise. I wish these gossiping fucks would leave me alone, not only did I have my two sisters in law to deal with, but now I had her father and her uncle adding in their two cents worth.

"Boy I'm telling you, my little girl can hold a mean grudge and she's got a mean streak a mile wide, you tell him Al."

"Yep, we've got the scars to prove it, remember that time she hid all the keys in the house and fucked up the phones so we couldn't call out?"

"Shit, I thought we were under attack or some shit." »

Tony and his side kick were eating it up, I was just sitting there keeping my cool, she'll be fine.

"Why did she do that?" Mikey was leaning over the back seat like a four year old at story time.

"We missed her school play." They laughed and shook their heads.

"What, that's it?"

"Yeah, it was like the second one in a row, plus some other things we missed in between."

"So how did you figure it out?"

"Her maid found the fucking contraband hidden in her closet, she'd gone around the house to all our hiding places and confiscated everything, she took all the keys and SIM cards and called the phone company, and had our calls forwarded to some throw away phone she bought."

"Why didn't you just use her phone to call out for help?"

"Said hers wasn't working either, I swear we thought we were under attack from some high tech faction." Alphonso was laughing his ass off.

"Two whole fucking days, my place isn't exactly within walking distance of my offices and shit and we didn't know where the fuck the threat was coming from so we hunkered down and went into protection mode, the little terror even played up the fear card all along too. Made me feel like shit because she couldn't go to some friend's party or some shit, while the whole time she had set the whole thing up."

"What did you do when the maid found the stuff?"

"We sat her down and tried to reason with her, what else can you do with a ten year old that can pull some shit like that off?" Rossi answered Tony.

"That's when Roberto and I first really realized what we had on our hands."

"Yep, and she's kept us on our toes ever since then, so boy I'm telling you, you're gonna pay for that stunt, watch your ass, I would at some point like to rock my grandchildren on my knees if you know what I'm saying."

I couldn't believe the leader of the mob world was sitting in my car gossiping about his daughter like a doting old woman after hitting a man that was out to kill him. I live in a fucked up world?

I listened to the four of them going on and on about what she might do to me, Tony and Mikey seemed to be having way too much fun thinking up ways that she could torture me, I wouldn't put it pass these two to help her out in any way with whatever she came up with, traitorous bastards.

"Mikey, how bout I tell Sophie how you were ogling Monica's ass."

"What...are you crazy, when did I do that, you trying to get my ass killed?"

I smirked at him before turning to the other one.

"If you and Lucy Ricardo over here put any ideas in Mouth's head I'm gonna be sharing a lot of shit with my sisters."

"My Anna would never believe that shit." Tony was all puffed up.

"She'd believe me if I tell her that you missed her birthday party so you could go watch the fight in Vegas."

"Bro you had that meet set up long before we realized that she was gonna throw the party on that particular Saturday, we couldn't pull out, that's what you said."

I polished my nails on my shirt as I grinned at him.

"That's cold bro, even for you, okay we won't put any ideas in her head, besides I don't think she needs our help." He was back to grinning like an ass, maybe I'll set them up anyway just for the fuck of it all, that'll keep them the fuck out of my business.

We pulled into the underground garage and I felt my heart rate pick up, what the fuck was I gonna find up there, knowing Mouth it would be snarky and insulting but beyond that I didn't think she would do anything harmful, like shoot me in the ass, besides she'd told me she loved my ass one of the times I'd been buried inside her.

That's right, I remembered my earlier counsel, no one had ever been inside her, and I had, so therefore she wouldn't treat me to the same horrors as everyone else.

The ride up was tense, the four henchmen were back to giving me looks, what the fuck ever. I think some of my confidence slipped when I turned the key in the door though.

Chapter 9

What the fuck?

"Mouth...how the fuck.....ma?"

What the fuck was going on around here? I walked through the door gearing up my nuts for the shit storm that was about to come, only to find that I'd been thwarted again.

"Seriously, are you fucking kidding me?"

"Shane Patrick Flanagan you watch your mouth."

My mother scolded me as she put what looked like a bowl of mashed potatoes on the table, my focus was on Mouth who had yet to say a word or even acknowledge my presence.

My two sisters came from the kitchen with more food in their hands while I looked around like I was in the twilight zone.

"How did you get out?"

"She called me."

"She called you, how did she do that?"

"Well actually she texted me and told me what you had done, shame on you, I thought I raised my son to treat a lady better than that."

"Ma...."

"Don't you ma me, you're lucky I don't let her dismember you as she's been threatening to do for the last three hours."

What the fuck, when the fuck had I lost control of my life and everything in it?

Yeah I could answer that one real easy, it happened the day I let a little spitfire into my office.

"Mouth?"

She spooned something in her mouth and looked right through me, the fuck? So that was her game, okay that wasn't so bad, the silent treatment, cool, I could deal with that.

"Who're these lovely ladies Flanagan?" I'd almost forgotten Rossis was here, I turned and made the introductions while my sisters and mother sat at the table.

Tony and Mikey joined them followed by Rossi and Alphonso; I sat next to Mouth and reached for some food. She must've told ma what we were up to, though my mom liked to pretend I was a legitimate business man, she knew the ropes, she'd been around grandpa long enough.

"So, she texted you and........?"

"Oh, she told me where she was and that you had some sort of control panel on the wall, we figured it was the keypad to open the door from the inside and so I gave her the code and voila. Then we decided to come over and cook a little late night something and keep her company."

"Ma....there's something wrong with that story, how do you know my code?"

"Son, please, I've known your code since you were in high school and I used to read your emails and stuff."

"What the fuck?" I felt my face heat up when I remembered some of the things I used to write to my squeezes back then.

"That's all kinds a messed up." I had to watch the cussing; she wouldn't let me get away with too much of that shit in her presence.

"That's what you get for using her birth date as your code idiot, some mob boss you are, she never read mine or Anna's, even Anna and I use to read your stuff sometimes. My sister Sophia smirked at me after divulging that shit.

I was not fucking amused though everyone else seemed to find this shit funny, all except Mouth who I noticed hadn't said one word since we sat down. She was even ignoring her father and uncle who didn't seem to find anything wrong with that, they carried on conversations around the table like there wasn't a silent person smack dab in our midst.

Okay I have to admit, that shit was.....scary, it's like waiting for the other shoe to drop, but not just any shoe, a steel toed boot.

"Mouth let me talk to you?" I whispered that shit, the last thing I needed was for any of these assholes to see me beg.

She didn't even bat a lash, it's like I hadn't even spoken. All throughout the meal it went like that, I was beginning to get frustrated as fuck, I mean if she screamed or came at me with a gun I could deflect that shit, but it was like I didn't even exist.

I have to say I don't like that shit one fucking bit, no way, no how.

The group moved to the living room after the table had been cleared and the dishes put away and still no word from Mouth.

I sat next to her on the couch, even put my arm around her, nothing, she didn't even tell me to fuck off, didn't try to move from under my arm. I didn't exist, fuck that shit.

I got up and dragged her from the room, in our bedroom I pushed her against the door and kissed her, or at least I tried, she just stood there, looking right into my eyes but with no response.

I tried again, biting into her bottom lip the way she liked, cupping her breast in my hand. Her nipple pebbled but she still didn't move or say anything. Fuck me, she was seriously pissed, I'm not sure I knew how to handle this shit.

I finally released her when I realized that she wasn't going to respond.

"So how long is the silent treatment gonna last, cause I gotta say, I'm not having much fun with this shit, you know I was right Arianna that was no place for you, so stop being a brat and talk to me."

Still nothing.

"Fine be that way, but understand I would do it again if I had to, to protect you from this shit I will do anything within my power so you be fucking mad all you want to." I left her standing there, finally working on my own mad. Fuck, I was just trying to protect her, was that so fucking bad, I don't care how fucking mad she got she wasn't getting involved in this life, fuck no.

I rejoined the others in the room who stopped all conversation when I sat back down. I gave them the finger, all except ma of course and settled down in my chair until I saw Mouth leave the bedroom with an overnight bag.

Oh fuck no.

"You ready Arianna?" Ma got up and went for her purse.

"What's going on?"

"She's spending the night and maybe the next few days with me until this cools down."

"No she isn't." I turned to look at her. "You're not leaving me...."

"She's not leaving you son, she just needs some time apart right now........"

I heard rushing water in my ears, that's all I heard before I lost my shit. Well at the time I didn't know I had lost my shit but apparently that's what happened.

The room was a fucking wreck when I came to my senses. The flat screen was shattered on the floor, the center table was up against one wall, the couch was on its side and who knows what the fuck else was broken, it looked like a tornado had passed through.

The men were standing around me with their hands on my shoulders, ma was holding Mouth back from getting near me, and it all came back into focus.

"You're not leaving."

"FINE, but I'm not talking to you asshole." She had tears in her voice as she ran to the bedroom and slammed the door.

Fuck, I think I scared Mouth; I haven't had one of these episodes since I was a kid, damn.

Mom came over and hugged me while the others got ready to leave.

"Are you sure she's safe here with him?" Rossi asked mom as they were headed to the door.

"She's the only one who is."

Chapter 10

I walked into the bedroom where she was lying on the bed fully clothed. I toed off my shoes and got in behind her.

Pulling her stiff body back against my front I held her tight.

"I'm sorry I scared you, but you will never leave me, be mad all you want but you be mad here, from now on that's where you belong, with me."

She didn't answer but I didn't care so much anymore, she had been afraid for me hadn't she, and she was here with me now, that was all the evidence I needed, she'll get over her mad soon enough, I hope.

Damn she had turned me into a fucking lunatic and we had only just begun.

I awakened sometime in the middle of the night with the boner from hell; I still had a tight grip on Arianna as she slept.

I wonder how seriously she would hurt me if I tried to fuck her right now, shit, she was asleep, if I did shit just right I could be in the pussy before she even awakened.

I started inching up her t shirt slowly, inch by inch, my fingers itched to touch her soft skin but I couldn't take the chance, I'll have to play after I was buried inside her.

How the fuck was I gonna get her wet if I couldn't touch her, shit, I didn't want to move, to reach over to the night table to get some gel, that might jar her awake too.

Fuck Flanagan you're a moron, I had a sinister grin as I used my hand to take some of the pre cum that was now running out my dick, ever so gently I smeared some over her slit, using the bare tips of my fingers, holding my breath, hoping she didn't wake up.

So far so good. I couldn't resist running my cock head up and down her slit from behind once before pushing in to her.

Fuck so soft, so hot.

Only when I was fully seated in her did I release my breath, her ass was tucked against my groin, held there with my hand on her belly.

I started a slow in and out, my dick swelling even more, I wanted to pound her so bad, but not yet, I knew it wouldn't be long before she woke up and I had to be ready for whatever she was gonna throw at me. The pussy was so good I didn't even mind a fight, shit.

Her ass twitched, her pussy tightened around my dick and she arched her back with a sigh. She pushed back against me, trying to take my root inside her, I let her have it.

My hand swept up towards her breast and I pinched her nipple as I sped up my hip movements a little more.

She was fucking back at me, good girl, see, I was worried for nothing. I nibbled her neck marking her, before turning her over onto her stomach.

Leaving her upper body flattened against the sheets, I lifted just her ass in the air, and plowed into her from behind, there was no other word for it.

She screamed into the bed as I grunted behind her, my dick couldn't seem to stop swelling inside her, I was hitting her spot with every plunge inside her, my hips were moving faster than I'd ever seen them, it was the most amazing fuck of my life.

"Shit Arianna, what the fuck have you done to me?"

My head felt like it would explode, the emotions in my chest could not be described, what....the ...fuck....?

I became a madman, at least that's how I would describe it, I bit and snarled all over her back, the need to mark her so strong, like some primitive being from another time. I have no fucking idea what came over me, all I know is that I needed to see my mark on her, to own her, possess her.

This was some Bram Stoker shit.

She whined beneath me as I attacked her body with mine, I wasn't fucking anymore, I was mating, where those words came from I don't know, but that's the thought that ran through my head.

I had to cum in her, deep in her, I didn't stop to think why, I just had to, it was almost as if I was compelled to do it.

I couldn't stop myself if I wanted to, I twisted my hip for a different angle, and on the next thrust I butted against her cervix.

It was soft, almost spongy, and felt amazing, and then my cock head pushed through into her womb.

"Fuuuuckkkk,Arghhhhhhhhh." I never came so fucking hard or so long in my life. All energy deserted me as she reached a climax beneath me, screaming, and writhing.

I dropped to my back like a wet rag, if Mouth decided to finish me off now I couldn't stop her, and if she knew what I had just done to her she would finish me.

I don't know how I knew but I'd just planted my kid in her, now to be fair, I didn't plan it, it seems almost like something pushed me to do it, I can't tell her that shit because she'd never believe me.

Fuck, I'm not telling her shit, she'd find out in a few months like everybody else does, I'll just have to keep an eye on her for both their sakes.

I turned to her pulling her back to me, her body was back to being a block of wood.

Alright, that's the way it is is it, tough. I forcefully pulled her back into my arms;

she actually struggled for a little bit before I tangled her up with my arms and legs.

"Seriously Mouth, I don't need you to talk to me to fuck you, you wanna give me the silent treatment go ahead, but in this room that shit is dead, now stop being a brat, and settle the fuck down."

Her body just stopped, just like that, I didn't trust it but she didn't move for the next five minutes, then I heard it, she was sniffling, what the fuck?

I turned her over and was gutted, she had fucking tears streaming down her face.

"No, no, no, no, no, baby...ssh, come on now, don't do that."

Have I mentioned how much I hate for the women in my life to cry, well seeing ma or the girls cry is nothing compared to this shit, you could fillet me with a hatchet, and that shit wouldn't hurt as much.

"Please, fuck, what did I do, did I hurt you, shit?" I was checking all over her body for injuries, it couldn't be the bite marks could it, I didn't think I was biting her that hard, hard enough to mark but not hard enough to break the skin, fuck.

She made a hiccupping sound as I pulled her little body closer to me.

"Tell me why you're crying; please tell me why you're crying baby."

"You didn't respect me."

"When, just now, Mouth...."

"No, before, when you locked me in the room, you don't respect me, you think I'm too stupid to handle myself, when I've been evading Carlo Stacco all this time on my own, I got all that information together and everything, but in the end you treated me like an air headed bimbo."

Fuck me, now she put it that way, I sounded like a real asshole, fuck, what the fuck was I supposed to do now?

"How can I fix this, huh, tell me what to do."

I didn't see the smirk that crossed her face, had I seen it I would've covered my balls and ran for cover.

Chapter 11

Prince of the City

Sucker, I'm glad his mom had let slip how much he hated tears, now I had him just where I wanted him, I knew the silent treatment wouldn't work for too long on his hard headed ass, the man had Alpha male stamped all over his shit, but there's always more than one way to skin a cat, now I had him in the palm of my hands, oh the possibilities.

I had to control my grin before I could answer him, couldn't give myself away had to make him sweat the little shit.

"I don't know that there's anything you can do, you made me look stupid in front your boys and my uncle and dad." I gave a little sullen shrug for effect.

You should see his face, if he could kick his own ass in that moment he would've. Meanwhile the tears are still flowing, hehehe.

"Come on now baby, stop crying you're fucking killing me here, whatever you want me to do I'll do it."

I let him hug me close, after all I loved his hugs and the sex, sweet merciful heavens, that shit was hot, maybe I should freeze him out more often because he went above and beyond on that one.

"I don't know, I'll think about it, let's just go to sleep okay."

"You done crying?" I nodded yes with tears on my cheeks. "You sure?"

Damn, he really hated tears, click, locked away for future use; life was so good to me. Don't laugh Ari he'd see through you in a flash if you do. But it was so hard not to, the big bad mobster freaked over a few tears, this was gonna be good. Though I'm not a simpering imbecile it wouldn't hurt to keep his ass in check every once in a while, and if I played my cards right, he'd never catch on that I was playing him. Sweeeeet.

Well that didn't last long, I had one day of free reign after my crying jag, a day where he treated me with kid gloves and let me do whatever I wanted, even going back to the club because I whined about how much I missed it. He wasn't too happy about it but he let me work a shift.

Then his natural bossiness kicked back in and it was all over. Damn.

Now he's on a tear because he heard through the grapevine that Carlo Stacco made a threat against me.

I walked into his study where he was once again ranting on the phone, his face a dark scowl as he sat behind his desk, shirt sleeves rolled up to his elbows , buttons undone to his chest.

Hmmm; if he ever caught on to how much I wanted him he'd be hard to deal with, better keep that to myself for a while yet.

I'd had no real idea who he was when I first came here, I knew of him of course, the youngest man in my father's profession so to speak, but I'd always pictured some heavy jowled out of shape blowhard, imagine my surprise when we first met.

He was the complete opposite to all that and I'd found myself day dreaming about him since then. I always swore I'd never end up with a guy like him, I wanted to get about as far away from this life as possible, but here I am, and if this nut had anything to say about it, here I'll be staying.

"They fuck with Mouth I would burn this whole mother fucking city down, no one fucks with what's mine and live, bring his bitch ass to me."

I rolled my eyes at his hot headed ass, if I ever see Carlo Stacco, which I planned to do soon, I'm going to kick his stupid ass, it's because of him that Don Vito had revoked my rights as a free thinking female.

He beckoned me over to his side, pulling me down into his lap as he gave orders to bring some guy name Taylor to him.

"I'm getting ready to leave." I told him as soon as he hung up the phone.

"Go where, where're we going?"

"To the club, I'm on tonight; they gave me back my shift."

"I can't go to the club right now I've got shit to do."

"Uhm, what does that have to do with the price of eggs, I'm going to work not hang out."

"You're not going without me and I can't get away right now."

"Shane....."

"Don't start no means no, now sit your hard headed ass right there and let me think."

I folded my arms and gave him the bitch please glare, which he ignored completely. Gah.

Chapter 12

Prince of the City

Okay, so Mouth is back to being her old pain in the ass self again. The furor from Stacco's hit is keeping my guys busy and now Ma has some wild hair about having everyone over for Sunday dinner, which means the fucking Rossi brothers.

To top it all off, Poppy has decided to leave his retirement paradise to pay us a visit. Fuck me, Poppy is a piece of work, I'm not sure about him and Mouth being in the same room together.

Fuck my life can nothing ever be simple? I think ma and the girls are in some sort of conspiracy with Mouth to make me lose my fucking mind. Every time I turn around she's on the phone with one of them, huh, not too sure about that turn of events. Though Mouth could out bitch the lot of them, those girls were hardcore, I'd have to keep an eye on that.

"Mouth could you please just listen to me and keep your ass at home, please, it will make my life so much easier if you would obey me."

"What am I a dog, and who died and made you the boss of me?"

"You're gonna get your ass spanked you keep this shit up, now let's go eat, it's getting late."

"Dinner's been ready."

"Yeah I know, I smelt it, smells good baby." I kissed her neck and squeezed her tit. Maybe I shouldn't start anything if we were planning on eating, but she always got me going with that damn mouth of hers.

I took her hand and rose from the chair heading into the dining room where she had the food covered to keep it warm. After seating her I took my seat across for her and dug in when she was ready.

"So anyway it's nice out I think I'll walk to the club." I dropped my fork on my plate, was I speaking a foreign language or some shit?

"Arianna, you...are...not....going......"

"Yes...I...am...."

You see this shit, right there, umph.

How the hell do I get her stubborn ass to behave without making her cry again, that shit makes my stomach hurt, I can't go through that shit again, I would be very happy if she never repeated that experience in this lifetime thank you very much, I didn't want her thinking I didn't care about her feelings though.

"Mouth, there are people looking to hurt you, I can't protect you if I'm not there and I can't be there right now."

"So let one of the others play body guard."

"I do not trust anyone else with your care when things are this hot, no fucking way. Don't pout baby it's not forever, just a few more days until I finish this shit up. Besides you're not supposed to be working at the club anymore remember?"

"You let me go last night."

Yeah that's because you caught me at a weak moment after those tears, I'm back on track now though. Of course I didn't say that to her, no sense giving her any more ammunition she'd just use it to make my life hell.

"Yeah well things have changed, you're not going, and that's final." She threw her fork at me. The fuck!

"I'm not your kid; you can't talk to me like that."

No but you might be carrying him, fuck if I'd let either of you be in danger. Again I kept that little tidbit to myself.

"Did you just throw a fork at my head?"

"Yes brainless, and if you keep stressing me I'll do worse."

"I'm stressing you; you've been nothing but a pain in the ass since you got here."

"That's easily fixed, why don't I take my ass with me?"

She got up and left the table.

"Mouth get back here." Of course she ignored me and kept going, I got up to follow.

"Mouth I'm not fucking around, if you leave here it's gonna be your ass."

"Oh yeah, how do you plan to stop me big bad mob boy?" She folded her arms and glared at me.

I looked her up and down lingering on her fuck hot ass and biting my lip, I felt my cock twitch in my pants.

"I could always fuck you into submission." I made a grab for her as she made a run for it. I caught up to her in the hallway and pinned her against the wall, rubbing my now fully erect dick against her ass.

"What now hotshot?" She gave a little wiggle of her hips and had my boy standing up and taking notice.

"Is this the only way to get you to listen?"

"I listen." I loved that little telltale hitch in her voice, she didn't think I noticed how she always melted whenever I put my hands on her. It was fascinating the way her body answered mine.

Taking her breasts in my hands I gave a squeeze before releasing one to pull down her shorts and taking off my belt.

I used the belt to tie her hands together and hold them above her head as she faced the wall. With my pants now open and my hard dick sticking out in front of me I used my cock head to tease her, sliding it up and down her ass crack to her pussy.

"Uhmmm, you're nice and soft and wet, you want me to fuck you baby, is that why you're messing with me, huh, you missed having this inside you?"

With one of her breasts in my hand, pulling on her nipple, I toyed with her pussy using just the tip of my cock.

She arched her back and tried to rub her pussy more forcefully against me. When that didn't work to her satisfaction she tried taking me in her hand and guiding me in from between her legs.

She got a smack on the ass for her trouble.

"Keep your hands up there." I put her hands back above her head on the wall.

I tapped the head of my cock against her pussy then rubbed it back and forth. Her juices were already starting to coat the head.

"You want this?" I whispered in her ear before taking the lobe between my teeth and sucking.

"Yes."

"Say it." I pushed two fingers inside her slowly, my thumb on her clit while still rubbing her with my cock from behind.

"Please...."

"Tell me."

"Please Shane, give it to me."

"What?" I bit her shoulder, sucking the skin until it turned red. Her pussy clenched around my fingers and she whimpered.

"Your cock, please give me your cock."

I slammed into her pulling her back so there was no space between us.

I fucked my girl like an animal, keeping her on her toes as I rammed her from behind.

"Oh shit....oh fuck.....please." She was climbing the wall, her nails scraping the paint. "Cum for me baby."

She moaned and twisted as I pounded her while fondling her tits and biting into her neck.

"Mine, mine, mine, fucking mine." My hips moved wildly against her ass.

"Please, Shane, too much."

"Never too much, never enough." I pulled her head back and kissed her hard biting her lip and tickling her clit until she convulsed and came, pushing back one last time, taking all of me inside.

When she came down I picked her up and headed for our bed taking the belt from around her wrists.

"I'm not through with you yet, when I'm done you won't even have enough energy to hold a thought."

I took her to bed and started all over again, eating her sweet pussy until she writhed with pleasure, her hands digging into my scalp as I held her legs open over my forearms.

I teased and prodded with my tongue before climbing over her and feeding her my cock. She choked and gagged on my length before she got her breathing under control and then she turned the tables on me.

Her tongue snaked out and licked my pre cum before she swallowed my cock, only to let go to tease me all over again. She was becoming a real cock tease. Playing with the head before licking down to the root of my shaft, sucking my balls into her hot mouth while digging her nails into my ass.

She made me so hot I pulled out of her mouth, raised her legs back over her head raising her ass and pussy up to me so I could feast.

I ate, licked, sucked, and growled in her pussy as her taste fed my hunger.

"Hold them."

She held her legs in position as I climbed to my knees, dick in hand, slippery from her saliva and my pre cum. I stroked it a few times watching as a string of pre cum hung from my cock to her pussy opening.

Holding her open with my thumbs, I guided my cock without hands into her. She grunted as I bottomed out, pinning her to the bed.

This angle did all kinds of amazing things, I was so deep, my cock felt huge as it plunged in and out of her.

She scratched my back as I took over holding her legs in place.

"Are you going to listen?"

"Shane...."

I pulled almost all the way out, teasing her with just the flared head of my meat.

"Please......"

"Answer me." I drove back in deep, then out again.

"You going to obey me Arianna?"

She tried pulling me in by grabbing my ass but I planted my toes in the bed, thwarting her efforts.

"Fucking do it....."

"No, answer me." I jabbed her a few times before going back to teasing.

"I'm.....I can't, I need it, please." She was almost in frenzy now, I tried to hold on, but it was hard when all I wanted to do was fuck the shit out of her.

"Are you going anywhere?"

She played me, I thought I had her but she clenched her pussy around my cock, twisted her hips in some kind of way that had me slipping and sliding back into the pussy, right where she needed me.

She bit into my neck as I pounded her, lost in her, so fucking lost in her.

"Fuck Mouth baby, I'll never get tired of this, of you, never."

I emptied my seed inside her as she came for me once more.

Chapter 13

I awakened to darkness, fuck; Mouth wore my ass out, shit. After that second time she'd sucked me back to readiness and then ridden me like nobody's business. The way she moved her hips and ass ...she fucking owned my cock.

I reached for her next to me, empty, cold sheets. Aw shit, I jumped from the bed and went in search of her but the stillness of the apartment already told me all I needed to know. There was no one here but me.

I tamped down the fear and lead with anger. If I got scared people might get hurt unnecessarily, it was better to hold on to anger.

I called downstairs and learned that she'd been gone for more than an hour; Taylor had been on ice for the last three, he could wait. I called the club and was told she'd never shown there, that's when fear kicked in.

I called every last one of my men and flooded the city looking for her.

She'd left on her own I was sure of that, but where the fuck was she?

La Principessa

I had to be really careful; the guards were on high alert ever since the old bastard had been taken out.

No one knew for sure who had done the deed, but it was widely suspected that Shane was behind the hit.

He'd filled me in on what had gone down, well some of it anyway, he was still working under the delusion that as a woman I shouldn't get involved in such things. He'd learn.

I scaled the outer walls and rolled into the shade. Counting down the seconds in my head, I waited for the strobe to pass before making a run for it to the side of the house.

I knew from recon that the lights were on special timers that made a sweep every five minutes less ten seconds.

Security was stationed in the back and front of the house leaving the sides unattended, maybe because the high walls and guard dogs were supposed to see to them.

I'd neutralized the dogs first; a little sleepy time steak was all I needed for that, they were three very well fed but heavily dosed dogs napping in the hedges beneath those walls.

No one will be looking for them since they only paid attention if the dogs gave an alert. Idiots.

I lifted the sleeve of the safety vest, shirt, whatever it is that Shane had given me, was that only days ago, it felt like forever.

He was going to be so mad, I couldn't think about that now though, I needed to concentrate or get my ass killed, one reassuring thing, if they got the jump on me, my father and uncle not to mention mobster boy, would tear them apart. Little solace if my ass was dead but it'll have to do.

I rock climbed my way up the side to the balcony on the second floor. Making sure there was no one in the room, I attached the window cutter to the pane of the window and silently cut out a circle before pulling it back with the piece of glass attached.

Next I reached my hand in and turned the lock in the window before sliding it ever so gently up.

I'm in.

Holding my breath I crept along the wall, it was still early, barely midnight, and since his old man had bought it in bed I'm thinking this wuss will probably be too scared to stay by himself for some time so he was probably surrounded by people. I might have to wait around here for a while.

Oh joy, that would just give Tommy Lucchese more reason to want to lock me away somewhere.

I used the heat seeking device I'd filched from Shane's safe room earlier to find the bodies in the house.

There were two goons sitting in what looked like a kitchen, in another room someone was on a phone, and in a bedroom some chick was riding someone, I'm guessing with their boss on high alert it had to be the esteemed Carlo Stacco getting his knob twisted.

I hefted the sack on my back as I checked the coordinates to the room. They were one floor up. Everyone else was on the second and first floor. The blue prints showed that the room Stacco was using was the attic room, only a bedroom and bathroom up there with a bird view window.

I had no idea when or if the chick was leaving, I also knew that if she left for a second I would have to use that window of time to do what I came here for, but then the discovery would be sooner than I wanted and I will be heading out that bird view window on the third floor. Shit.

I had no choice, I was sure if I made it out alive Flanagan would never let me see the light of day again, it was now or never.

I silently made my way from floor to floor, the two in the kitchen were no problem they were too far away to give me worries for now, it was the one on the second floor with me that could pose a problem.

Thankfully he was yapping away on the phone, when he paused I stopped and held my breath as he told the person on the other end to carry on, he thought he'd heard something but it was nothing, I released my breath and kept crawling along the hall way. The damn place was lit up like a Fourth of July fireworks show.

There was movement in the attic room as I watched the screen. This was a neat little toy, maybe I'd keep it for future endeavors, that's if Lucky Luciano let me live.

It looked like chicky was gathering her things, good. She headed into the other room which looked like the bathroom and turned on the shower.

Damn this thing was good.

I hurried my pace as I was out of danger range so to speak. I'd really wanted to have a little chat with Stacco before but circumstances didn't let me, a girl had to do what she had to do.

Taking the sack from my back I pulled out what I needed as I entered the room, he was lighting up a cigarette when he bought it. There wasn't even a sound made. Female my ass, I didn't even shake.

I made my way back down the way I'd come, the adrenaline hadn't kicked in as yet, I was still in protect me mode, had to get out.

I had no idea how long the shower would last but I didn't need to be around to find out. The dogs were making waking up noises when I reached the wall. Damn, how long had I been in there?

I scaled the wall and hot footed it to my car which I'd parked about a mile away. I ran full out as I heard car doors slamming from the direction behind me.

My car was hidden in a copse of trees off the side of the road, imagine my surprise when I got there and saw the lone figure standing with arms folded.

Oh shit, I turned to head back from whence I came, I'll take my chances with the goon squad thank you very much. One pissed off Gambino or three inept goobers, easy.

"Get your ass back here."

Well damn, my shoulders slumped as I strolled over to him.

"Funny meeting you here." I tried a smile; I guess it didn't work when the scowl on his face got darker. He studied me for a minute before pulling me into his chest and kissing the shit out of me. Now the adrenaline kicked in, and I did the most female stupid shit thing in the world. I burst into tears. Why the fuck was I crying?

His strong arms wrapped around me tight as he soothed me.

"Hush baby, it's okay, you're okay now. Did you do what you came here to do?"

"Uh huh, I had to Shane, please understand that...."

"We'll talk about that later; right now let's get out of here."

"You came alone?"

"The boys are around, let's go."

He put me in the passenger seat and buckled me in before coming around to the other side.

"You know you fucked up right?"

"I know...."

"No Mouth, you really fucked up, I can't trust you, how can I be with you if I can't trust you?"

"What?" My heart started to hurt, like seriously hurt, what was he saying here?

"Since we seem to want two different things I think we might have to go our separate ways, I can't go through what you put me through tonight again, and you need to prove something so I say we call it quits before we take this any farther."

Someone was screaming I don't know who, but my heart hurt like a son of a bitch and I wished whoever it was would stop; the sound was haunting, full of pain, so much pain.

Chapter 14

Prince of the City

"Fuck me." I pulled over and turned to her. She was holding her tummy and screaming in pain.

"What the fuck Mouth, you hit, let me see." I tried pulling her hands away; she latched on to me, her arms like a cobra as she clung to me and that fucking scream. If they'd hurt her I'd bring them back from the dead and shoot their fucking asses.

"Arianna let me see. Fuck." She wasn't moving; I had to forcefully push her away to get a look at her middle.

My heart was in my fucking throat, she was scaring the shit outta me. No blood.

"Where you hit baby tell me?" She grabbed my hand and put it over her heart as her screams became whimpers.

Her heart! She can't be heart shot. I tore open the shirt she wore and released a breath when I saw the bullet proof shirt underneath.

Okay, okay, she wasn't hit, so what the fuck?

Oh shit ...I'd set her off. I pulled her over the console and into my lap.

"Calm down baby, it's okay, ssh, ssh...it's okay."

She hauled off and slugged my ass. The fuck?

"Don't you threaten me again you fucking bastard." She pummeled me but good, I was ducking her little fists the best I could in the confines of the car.

What'd I say, bat shit crazy.

I caught both her hands in mine, pulling her face close to me.

"Listen you, I've had enough shit out of you, when we get home I'm gonna wail your little ass. After I got through being scared out of my fucking mind and having my men search the whole damn city looking for you, I finally clicked into the fact that you'd gone after Stacco. Following a hunch I called up your little cohorts and my sisters felt guilty enough to let me in on your little trick, control me with fucking tears will you? All so you can get your own way and put your ass in danger, payback's a bitch isn't it?"

"You....you did that on purpose...you...you.....arggghhhhh."

I laughed which only pissed her off more.

"Calm your little ass down you're in enough trouble as it is don't make it worse on yourself." She got real quiet, I'm not sure I trusted that either crazy lady was kinda unpredictable.

I put her back in her seat and continued home. My guys should be finished with clean up back at Stacco's hideout. Tommy's sneaky ass was lucky he'd given up what she'd been up to. Apparently while she was supposed to be in school she'd been out following Stacco and his detail around. She'd known his whereabouts this whole time, or at least for the last couple weeks. Smart fuck.

I pulled into the garage where Mikey and Tony were waiting, the others must've gone to tie up loose ends, they knew what to do so none of this blew back on us, I didn't want Stacco's body found too soon after his father bought it, the fucking Feds will probably think they had another gangland war on their hands and be all in my business, I didn't have time for that shit. I had one dirty cop to deal with and then I was taking it easy for a while.

"Hey champ how's it going?" The two asses high fived her as we left the car.

"You okay there lil brother?"

"What the fuck are you talking about now yenta?"

"We were behind you when you pulled over; we thought you might need us but uh...." The fuckers started laughing. I guess they'd seen Mouth beating the shit out of me in the car.

"Everything taken care of?"

"Yep, by the way Ari, that was cold."

"How'd she do him?"

"Bow and arrow. One right through the neck pinned the fucker to the bed. We let the female live she didn't see anything and she's pretty much catatonic, we'll keep her on ice for a few days just to be on the safe side but I don't think she'll be repeating this story anytime soon. The guards were neutralized, place was cleaned, he's in and out."

"Good, you two coming up or you heading home, I'm for bed it's late."

"Nah we'll catch you tomorrow, I'm sure the girls are waiting to hear what happened."

"Yeah about that, could you two try to control your wives? What would've happened if she'd been hurt?"

"But she wasn't and you can't really blame the girls you know your woman is.....different....."

"Hey I'm right here....."

"Sorry Ari, no disrespect, don't pull out the gun or whatever weapon you're packing." Mikey was a real comedian.

"Get the hell outta here."

"What about Taylor?"

"Let the fucker sweat it out some more."

"Tomorrow then." They headed for their car as I led Mouth to the elevator.

I took her upstairs and looked her over to make sure there was nothing wrong with her, I know she'd never killed anyone before, I also knew how the first time felt.

"How do you feel?"

"I think I got the shakes."

I poured her a cognac and made her down it before running her a bath and taking care of her.

I put her to bed and held her as she calmed down from her adrenaline rush.

Just before she fell asleep I whispered in her ear.

"Tomorrow I'll deal with your stubborn ass, you do this shit again we're gonna have problems, I understand why you felt you had to do this yourself, but you don't do shit like this, I told you this already but you don't hear so good so tomorrow we'll go over it again."

She huffed and sighed, punched her pillow, glared at me and finally tried to leave the bed.

I pulled her back into my side.

Chapter 15

La Principessa

I woke up over mob boy's legs while he prepared to spank me, oh hell no. I tried twisting away off his lap but he kept me in place with one hard hand in my back.

"You up...Good." He brought his hand down hard on my ass. I think I yelled more from the surprise than the actual pain, that hadn't set in yet.

"What.....I......say.....goes." He punctuated each word with a smack to my bare ass that burned.

This fucker had lost his mind.

"Stop it Shane that hurts." I tried kicking up my legs but he just wrapped his around them somehow and kept wailing away on my ass.

"Pretty sure it's supposed to, now be a good girl and take your punishment."

I cried, I begged, I pleaded, but to no avail, I was never so embarrassed in my life, how could he? I was crying real tears and plotting his death.

What reason was I going to give Pia for killing her son?

He rubbed my sore behind when he was done, all the while laying down the law, all I heard was a lot of you can't do this, don't do that, I wasn't listening, I was plotting my own revenge.

Prince of the City

She was sniffling and sulking when I finally let her up, my hand hurt so I know her ass must be on fire, that's what she got for disobeying me and going off to do shit on her own.

I hugged her to me and cuddled, she was like a little kitten curled up on my chest as I laid back on the bed, bringing her with me.

"Mouth....."

"Why do you always call me that, you never call me anything sweet.....?”

"That's not true; I call you sweet things all the time."

"No you don't, you call me Mouth or you're always lecturing me about something, you never say anything nice to me, it's always Mouth don't do this or Mouth don't do that."

I rolled us over so I could look at her.

"Baby that's just not true, I always call you by endearments don't I?" I thought I did, was she right, shit now she had me questioning myself.

I brushed the hair back from her face and dried her tears. How was it possible to feel so much for someone, someone you hardly knew, but couldn't wait to get to know, because I just know in my gut that life with her will be perfect, no matter what.

I know that the more I get to know her the more in love with her I'll be, her strength fucking scares me. She thinks like a fucking general leading his troops like.....me. Fuck.

"Baby do you understand why I don't want you involved in this shit, why you can't be, this is not a place for you."

"Shane I'm not a gangster okay, this was personal, it's not like I'm gonna go around the city shooting people and shit, or pulling off heists, though on a side note I think the girls and I would make an awesome team.......yeah maybe we should organize......"

"Fuck me, no, don't even joke about that, could you just act like a girl for once, I don't want my wife acting like a dude, she has to be feminine."

If she wanted to give me ulcers she was well on the way, the thought of them hatching some plan to do some stupid shit was enough to turn every hair on my head grey, I know she was only kidding though, at least I hope she was.

I was about to say something to her when her fist connected with my eye.

"Ow, fuck, Mouth....come back here." She'd made a run for it. My fucking eye was throbbing but that didn't stop me from running after her. Would it be sick to admit that I'm proud of my woman? She's got balls of fucking steel, my perfect match, that didn't mean I wanted her playing Bonnie to my Clyde, I just can't do that shit, her ass will stay home and that's that.

"I see spankings don't work, next time I'm getting the belt for your ass, where are you?"I found her in the kitchen rummaging through the freezer; she threw a bag of veggies at me.

"Here, put that on your eye, at least no one can see what you did to me." She laughed like this shit was funny.

"Were you ever tested?"

She cocked her head at me, “For what?"

For what? Fucking nut job.

I put the cold bag against my face for some relief, I don't think I'd been clocked in the face since I was a teen or some shit,what the hell did I get myself into.

"Why'd you run out the room, I wasn't done with you yet?"

"You come anywhere near my ass again and I'll shoot you, as for your feminine wife tell that bitch I say run for the hills cause you're stuck in the dark ages."

"It doesn't matter what you say, what happened last night will never be repeated, you're done with this shit, I'm serious Arianna, no more."

She rolled her eyes and looked through the fridge coming out with an apple.

"You want one?"

"For breakfast?"

"I'm not feeding you, you spanked me, and now you want me to feed you, I'll go all Delores Claiborne on your ass."

"Who?" What the fuck?

"There's a mobster with that name, what kinda fucked up shit is that?"

"Never mind clueless, it's a movie, one of these days we'll watch it together."

"I'm not watching any chick flicks that shit is out."

"You want me to hang around here you'll watch what I watch and you'll like it mister."

She was mighty feisty for someone who just got her ass beat, which meant it didn't do shit. Damn. She'd be back on the streets getting into shit as soon as my back was turned.

"You got anymore personal vendettas I should know about Mouth?"

"I'm thinking very seriously about doing your ass in, why?"

I just gave her a look because for all I know crazy lady could be serious.

"Where'd you learn to use a bow and arrow anyway?"

"It's my weapon of choice, years of archery classes baby."

"I thought shooting people in the ass was your forte?"

"Nah, that's just a warm up, speaking of which, how's Jimmy?"

Fuck dinner Sunday, Mouth, James, Poppy and the two old mobsters, fuck my life.

"Since you're not making me breakfast lets go back to bed."

Crazy lady stared me down, I waited her out.

"I'd straight up Bobbit you."

Okay even I knew who that was, she bit into her apple and grinned at me, amazing, from tears to a face punch to threats, this was the woman I wanted to spend my life with. I needed my head examined.

"What're you doing today?"

"I'm going shopping with your mom and sisters."

"Fine I'll get the car ready for you when you're ready."

"I can drive myself thank you very much."

"No, you can't...and don't bother arguing because it's either that or you stay home."

She threw her half eaten apple at me.

I barely caught it before it connected with my face. I gave some serious thought to lobbing it back at her but figured she'd probably gut me, crazy fuck.

"What's it gonna be?"

"Listen you ancient relic, between the four of us we can pretty much find our way around a gear shift, we don't need nor do we want a babysitter."

I ignored her and went to get some eggs to make breakfast for both of us; she'd turned me into a fucking sap.

La Principessa

He's so adorably cute when he's flustered, I like keeping him on his toes, no matter how cute he was I'm still gonna get him back for the stunt he pulled in the car last night and for the spanking. I figure I had the spanking coming, he's a pigheaded son of a bitch after all, but that stunt was over the top, no way I could let him get away with that.

Like Pia said, I had to train him early. There'd be hell to pay if he ever found out that his mom and sisters and even his brothers in law were giving me pointers on how to handle him.

I'd got him good with that endearment thing, he hated feeling like he wasn't taking care of me or doing everything he was supposed to, I could so use that in my favor.

He thinks he's the big bad mafia don, but I'll soon show him who's boss.

Life was sure going to be interesting around here, especially when he found out I was going to Chicago for a while.

I couldn't wait to have that conversation, oh joy.

The End

Join me next time for more Mouth and Shane in Beautiful Assassin

"Mouth go put something on."

"What, why, there's no one here but us?"

"There're windows all over the place go put something on now."

"Hey Vito Andolini, I can't put anything on because my as hurt; and if down here is bare what's the point in covering up up here?

The Assassin

By

Jordan Silver

Chapter 1

I made us eggs and toast for breakfast as Mouth toddled around the kitchen, she didn't sit to eat which clued me in to how much her ass must hurt along with other things.

"Mouth go put something on."

"What, why, there's no one here but us."

"There're windows all over the place that's why, go put something on now."

"Hey Vito Andolini, I can't put anything on because my ass hurt, and if down there is bare what's the point in covering up up here, besides the kitchen window faces the back deck which you have covered in a forest, we're fifty stories high who the hell can see anything?"

"There're buildings all around here, who knows what fuck is out there with binoculars or some shit, plus the fucking Feds probably have me in their cross hairs and I'd be fucked if I have their greasy asses jacking off to my woman, now go put some shit on."

Instead of listening to me, the little terror actually leaned over the table with her ass to the window.

Now see, ma's met her, she knows, there's no way she doesn't know that this girl drives me insane, so if I chucked her ass off the deck ma would maybe understand.

I held my peace, why bother, she wouldn't listen out of spite anyway, that's her thing.

I put the dishes in the dishwasher after we were done because the mouthy one said until her ass healed she was on strike, she snubbed her nose at me and pranced down the hallway to her shower. I gave her five minutes before I pounced.

With my pajama bottoms discarded on the bedroom floor, and my already hard cock in my hand for a stroke I followed her into the shower.

Before she could wash the shampoo out of her eyes and get water out of her mouth to blast me, I had one hand around her throat and the other on her pussy.

"You want to be bad?"

"Oh shit"

"Let's play tough girl."

Bending my knees slightly I pushed up and in, whatever sound she made was cut short by my hand around her throat as I pulled her down on my cock by her hip.

"Hands against the wall, assume the position."

She placed both hands flat against the wall as the water cascaded over both of us from four separate angles.

"Will you ever listen pretty girl?" I whispered in her ear.

"Yes..." Her voice held that breathy sigh that I liked.

"Is this the only time you obey me...huh...when I'm fucking you?" I gave a deep hard jab that had her scrabbling for purchase against the slick wall.

"Lean your head against your hands and push that ass back I feel like doing you deep."

She did that shit quickly; with my hand still around her throat and one on her ass, I pounded her pussy with punishing strokes, not enough to hurt, but enough that she'd feel me for at least the next two days.

"Ahh...fuck...you sadist..." She was pushing back against me twitching her ass as she fucked herself on my cock, I kept up a nice steady pace digging deep, watching my cock as it went in and out her pussy juices covering my shaft. Pulling out I knelt behind her and licked and gently kissed her reddened ass cheeks. Poor baby; I took little swipes with my tongue around the cheeks of her ass, blowing soothing cool air against her abused ass, damn I hadn't realized I'd been hitting her that hard, I'm lucky she hadn't retaliated more forcefully then again knowing her crazy ass I'm probably not in the clear yet.

"Please Shane, put your mouth on me."

"Where?"

"You know where, please, don't make me beg."

"No, tell me...."

Crazy lady grabbed me by the top of my head and lead my mouth to her pussy.

I had no choice but to comply, besides it was no hardship to eat her sweet pussy, her taste was in me now, her scent, her feel, everything about her had become a part of me.

"Uhhhhh...ummmmmm.... so good." She didn't let go of my hair as she sought her orgasm cumming on my tongue. I was up and in her before she was finished screaming out her pleasure pounding away at her pussy until I remembered that she might be carrying my kid, and then I slowed down with a sinister grin.

I pulled out yet again because suddenly I needed to be closer to her; I turned her in my arms and kissed her softly while entering her once again. I washed her hair as she rode my cock, her arms and legs holding me tight. "I love being inside you baby, it's like coming home, like all the good things in my life wrapped up in one little package, and your pussy is unbelievably sweet."

She trembled at my words and sought my mouth with hers so we shared a kiss that took our breaths away. Instead of the fast race to the finish that I'd expected, we came together in a soft sweet ending.

She did wobble out the shower though so I guess my work was done.

"What time are you supposed to go shopping?"

She looked at her watch.

"Like an hour."

She was pulling on low rider jeans and a sweater, my heart lurched when I recognized the sweater as one of mine it was way too big but sexy as fuck on her. What was it about seeing her in my shit that was such a fucking turn on?

I threw a wad of cash and a credit card across the bed at her.

"What's this, oh my God, how much money is in here?"

"It's in stacks of ten thousand how many stacks you got?"

"One, two, three, four, five...you threw seventy thousand dollars and a credit card at me?"

"What, not enough, here take more." I threw another stack at her, the fuck I know about women and shopping all I know is that dad always said never tell a woman about her spending habits and peace will reign.

"I distinctly remember telling you that my coochie was not for sale."

"What the fuck..."

"When you give a woman that you've only known for a short while lots of money after you've fucked her, there's a name for it."

"Are you fucking insane Mouth...what the fuck am I saying, yes you are, first of all don't say that shit about yourself again, and secondly you know the deal, how many times have I called you my wife?"

"You can't just tell me I'm your wife you mook, and you don't just throw money at a woman like that unless she's a cheap..."

I grabbed her hand and pulled her behind me to the wall safe. Opening it I removed the box I had hidden there since the morning after I believed I'd impregnated her.

Opening it I turned to her. "You see this? Four point two million dollars, this makes that petty cash in your hands insignificant, still think you're my whore?" I just pushed the ring onto her finger.

"What the hell are you doing? You didn't ask."

"Who can ask you anything? With you I have to just tell or do because you don't listen for shit."

"Hey, that's not true...."

"Mouth do you not see yourself? You're a pain in the fucking ass, now that that's done I don't want to hear anymore about whores and shit...you like it?"

She looked at the rock I had just forced on her hand.

"Four point two...I can't walk around with this shit on my hand..."

"You ever take that off it's going to be your ass just saying."

"Listen Captain twit, stop with the threats and go do something about that eye, it look a mess."

Shit I forgot she'd clocked me, I probably had a shiner by now oh fuck Mikey and Tony, shit.

"We clear on the money shit?"

"Clear." She nodded her head once for emphasis.

"And the marriage deal?"

"Working on it, still not sure I want to spend the rest of my life dealing with your brand of insanity."

"My...fuckingpainintheassnutjob." I mumbled under my breath because I did not want to deal with any more of her shit, I had to go, there was shit to do.

I went out to the living room to get my phone that I'd left there to call the guys. They were already on their way with ma and the girls.

I went back into the room to get my shit for the day, nothing.

I looked all around the room for my shit, searched the living room, den, every room in the house, my favorite piece was missing. Fuck, I'm a superstitious fuck, can't leave without it.

Okay, there're only two of us in here and no one came in, I know sneak girl hid them.

"Mouth what the fuck, where's my shit?"

"What shit?"

"My piece, my keys, the shit I had sitting here five minutes ago."

"I have no idea of what you speak."

Her lying ass kept a straight face as she looked me dead in the eye and spewed that shit.

"Mouth stop fucking around."

"And where pray tell are you going Giuseppe?"

"I gotta see a guy about something."

"I don't think you should do that."

"What the fuck, why not?"

"Well, seeing as you only have one working brain cell I think you might be a danger to yourself and others."

This fucking girl.

"Mouth your ass cooled down already did it? Give me my shit before I belt you one."

"Ha, how you plan to explain that black eye to the peanut gallery anyway?"

I got a fresh pair of aviators off the shades rack in my closet.

"Nice." She cat whistled at me, crazy nut.

"The others are coming up you ready?"

"Yep, I got cash, cards and my glock."

"Your...? Mouth give me the gun."

"No way are you bent, I never go anywhere without my backup."

"What the bow and arrow won't fit in your bag? You won't be needing it, your detail will have you covered."

"Uh huh, so why don't you go without yours?" I think I had enough time to strangle her ass before the others got here, just barely but I could do it.

"Where's my shit Mouth?"

She shrugged at me and ran, when I caught her laughing ass in the living room and snatched her purse she had my shit and half an apartment in there. Women.

I was heading out the door since I'd decided I would meet the boys downstairs, I still wasn't talking to ma and the girls they'd fucked up so I didn't want to see them, I did decide to take my life in my hands though.

"Oh yeah, you might want to see about a pregnancy test while you're out, I think I knocked you up the other night."

She looked at me stymied.

Uh huh, maybe I'd found something to calm her little ass down after all we'll see.

Chapter 2

I slammed the door after my little bombshell and stood outside waiting for her reaction.

"One two three..."she came flying through the door, skidding to a halt when she saw me leaning against the wall.

"You take that back."

"What, my seed, I think it might be too late for that." I smirked at her and to add insult to injury, I pulled her towards me, putting my hand flat against her stomach.

"I think he's right about...here." I pressed my fingers into her tummy softly.

She stomped her foot pissed way the fuck off so I decided to fuck with her even more.

"Watch that stomping shit before you dislodge my kid." Oh this was going to be fun.

She punched me in the gut and tried to head butt me; see what I mean? Crazy fuck.

"You hit like a girl." I had to hold her hands behind her back to keep her from dismembering me. While I had her there I might as well steal a kiss, or two, so I did. Sweet.

"You can't know that, there's no way you can know if you knocked me up or not." She was out of breath from my kisses but still had a whole lot of fight left in her.

"I had an epiphany or some shit, I'm telling you, its real."

"What the hell are you talking about?"

"When I was fucking you the other night, I felt it, something, I don't know what the fuck, I just know that I knocked you up. Besides, what did you think was going to happen if you kept letting me hit it without a cover?"

"I don't know, that first time you blindsided me, and after...after I just didn't think about it okay. I can't have a baby right now Shane."

"And why the fuck not?"

"Because I just can't." Arms folded, she looked at me like I was responsible for all the wrongs in the world.

"Well if I'm right and he's already in there then it's a done deal, nothing you can do about it now."

"I will kill you in your sleep mob boy."

"You saying you don't want my kid?" I scowled at her, what the fuck, was she seriously rejecting my kid?

"I didn't say that twit, I just said not now, I have things to do..."

"So you do want to have my kids?" I grinned like the fucking sap I'd become.

"Kids, how did we go from one imaginary child to many?"

I looked down at her hand with my ring on it; at least she hadn't taken it off.

I thought it best to change the subject for now since she looked like she was about to go ape shit on my ass.

"You didn't tell me if you like your ring, I thought it was perfect."

"It is perfect, but shit Shane, almost five million dollars."

I pulled her in for a kiss. "I would've spent more, my girl deserves only the best. Now you want to tell me why you think you can't have my kid now?" So much for changing the subject; great now she's got me confusing my own fucking self.

She looked away guiltily; fuck me.

"Mouth...." I was starting to get a sick feeling in my gut.

Just then we heard the elevator and my family came out, the women dressed pretty much like Mouth, the two boobs in Armani suits.

"Later Eddie boy, we'll talk later."

I'd forgotten all about my eye until my sister-in-law Michael mentioned it.

"Nice shiner there bro another knockout bout with the champ?"

"Oh Shane, we heard all about you getting beat up, my poor boy did the mean little girl hurt you?"

Ma kissed my cheek while stifling laughter.

The bigmouthed duo was cracking themselves up and my adoring sisters were smirking. Everybody was a damn comedian around here.

"Very funny let's go."

"I need my purse and jacket." She ran back inside to get her stuff.

"So why did she clock you this time?"

"What are you, a reporter? Why don't you see to your own wife? I seem to remember Sophie kicking your ass a time or two, moron."

"Nah, that was Tony and Anna, me and my Sophie don't engage in that type of behavior."

"Yeah, who was it that had a fat lip and a broken nose six months ago?"

"Never mind that, we were talking about you."

"No we weren't."

Tony thank God was busy sucking face with Anna so he had no time to stick his nose in my business, ma and Sophie had gone into the apartment after the terrible one, so it was just me and the yenta.

We heard screams and laughter followed by 'Anna get in here and oh Shane you did good' that last one was from ma. I guess they'd finally seen the rock on my baby's hand; it was kinda hard to miss.

I distracted the Bobsie twins with talk of work, there's no way I was discussing weddings and shit with their nosy asses.

"Anything out of Taylor yet?"

"Plenty, I hear he's been talking up a storm after getting his knees busted."

"Anything of importance?"

They looked at each other before Tony turned to me with a serious look.

"You want to do this now with the girls here?"

I stood up from the wall studying him; we knew each other very well so I could read between the lines.

"That serious huh."

"Yeah you could say that."

Okay, I know my people, from Mikey's body language I figure he knows

I'm going to lose my shit when I hear whatever it is they have to say.

"Just tell me this one thing, is my woman in any danger?"

"In direct danger no, not really."

"You sure? Be very sure that whatever it is you have to tell me does not in anyway pertain to her safety."

"Nah we would've told you already if that was the case bro you know that."

Yeah I knew that I just wanted to be sure, I could deal with all the shit out there just not with anyone fucking with her.

Steven Taylor is a dirty cop who's been playing both sides of the fence. He'd been feeding my guys Intel, which he wasn't the only cop I owned, I owned plenty, some in very high positions even up to the mayors' office and beyond, but it seems he'd also been selling information to the Staccos.

I inherited these dirty fucks from Poppy; ever since I've been trying to go legit there've been grumblings. If I went legit a lot of these guys would lose their kickbacks, which were sometimes more than they made in a year according to what they did for me, it wasn't cheap to turn a blind eye these days.

We went down together in the elevator ma and the girls oohing and aahing over the ring and throwing around wedding questions, ma was already planning shit. That's my girl.

Mouth was still giving me looks but not saying anything in front of the others. I didn't say anything either because I figured we needed to talk first, I wanted to know why she seemed afraid to have my kid.

Drawing her stiff form under my arm I whispered in her ear." Be good okay, I'll see you later, have fun shopping."

She softened a little when I kissed her temple softly as the doors opened.

There were three cars on them with Tommy in charge that fuck. I'm sure mouth will have a lot to say about the heavy security but she'll have to get over that shit.

I watched as they left the underground garage before climbing into my own car with the boys.

"Tell me."

"Ricci's on the take." Tony took the lead this time.

"Say what now?"

"Yeah very recent, it seems our boy Taylor had his own sideline going, he's been taping conversations in the club, well some areas anyway, he was only able to plant one listening device."

"We sweep every week." I gotta deal with this bullshit now on top of everything else? Fucking dirty cops no loyalty and no ethics whatsoever, why the fuck Poppy ever got into bed with them in the first place was a mystery. I say just shoot the fucks on sight if they get in your way and be done with it.

"He moves it around accordingly, anyway we have Ricci talking to someone we believe is James Foster, the conversation took place right around the time he came in and you took care of him. I think from the sounds of it it's some kind of jealousy thing, you love Arianna, she's trying to get with you..."

"I thought you said this didn't involve Mouth?"

"It doesn't not really, well not in anyway that we can't handle; the bigger issue is what Taylor might've gotten on his surveillance. The Ricci thing is just female drama."

"You think that makes a fucking difference? So what, she brought James in to cause static or was there something else?"

"Something like that, from what we heard, and the shit's a little convoluted, you'll probably make more sense of it when you hear it yourself, but she seems to have gone around the bend. Her thinking's all whacked.

"You think? If the trick thought to go up against me she's not just fucked in the head she's got a fucking death wish. What did she expect him to do to Mouth anyway?

"Um...take her out to hurt you, but like I said we knew there was no way that shit was going to happen. Mouth is safe bro, you've got her covered from all angles nothing to worry about on that score."

I tightened my fist, my first inclination was to turn around go get mouth, take her home and lock her away somewhere. I had about as much chance of pulling that shit off as I did pulling down the space needle one handed. Fuck.

Pulling out my phone I called her anyway just to hear her voice.

"What Falconi?"

"That fucking mouth, where are you mob girl?"

"In the car on the way to Nordstrom where I plan to spend every dime of your money before going off to Neiman Marcus and Hermes to get started on your card."

I guess she thought that would scare me.

"Spend as much as you like there's more where that came from, I'll see you later baby." I hung up on her snort.

"Where's Ricci now?"

"She's at the club."

"It's time to clean house, if the twat betrayed me in this who knows what else she's been up to."

"So far it's just her and the cop, but you already know the cops are trying to keep you in the mix, legit business is no benefit to them."

"We're almost there anyway, I'm still gonna keep my hand in in some things but it's time to clean this shit up. I think Mouth would like that."

"You are so gone." Mikey snorted at me.

"A real man thinks about his woman's happiness, only a fucking ape wouldn't, now you two are a whole other story, you're just plain whipped."

"And what are you, getting married and shit, she's domesticating you, next thing you know you'll be wearing an apron and cooking her breakfast in bed."

"That's Tony's deal." Mikey and I razzed him a little because he really was such a wife, I'd be fucked if Mouth was going to turn me into het stooge.

"Hey, it keeps my girl smiling, fuck you two. Assholes, you don't know shit."

Mikey and I laughed, it was good to ease the tension that had risen, soon enough we'd be knee deep in somebody's blood. Fuck I'm tired. I just wanted to take my mouthy one and hide from the rest of this shit for a while, but the chances of that happening anytime soon were slim to none.

First because with her I doubt I'd ever have another moment's peace for the rest of my days and two I still had a fuck load of shit to clean up before my kid was born.

Chapter 3

I didn't spend too much time on Taylor, I just had one question for him and that was what info he'd sold to the Staccos, now with father and son gone that organization would be over run by the violence of underlings trying to be top dog unless I moved in and dismantled the shit, which is what I planned on doing anyway.

The next few months were going to be hell with me trying to clean shit up in my backyard. I'll have the cops and the fucking criminals breathing down my neck, if I could get some of the others on board to go legit things might be easier. A few of the old timers were already on board, but there were still a few more who didn't see the benefit. I'll make sure and show them the error of their ways. I'm going to make this city safe for my son or daughter if it fucking kills me.

By the time Taylor's carcass was being nibbled on by fish in the deep, I was on my way to deal with Ricci.

My phone went off alerting me to a call from Tommy, my heart went haywire before I even answered the call.

"What is it?"

"Someone made a play, we're headed to your family estate, meet you there."

"Where's my fucking woman?"

"She's safe, they're all safe but I'm taking them in until we know more, this old boy was from back home."

"The fuck?" My heart actually fucking hurt it was beating so hard.

I hung up and called Mouth, I needed to year her voice for myself, be sure she was okay.

"You okay?"

"Well hello to you too."

Fucking girl could never do what I expected.

"Arianna stop fucking around, are, you, okay?"

"We're fine the girls are all excited, except for Pia, I think she might need a sedative or something, nothing much really happened, I just happened to recognize someone from back home; I didn't think he was here for the scenery so I alerted your goon squad and voila. We've been herded like sheep and being packed off to God knows where. Needless to say, we are not amused, there's a pair of Loubotins with my name on them."

"I'm coming to you, just do what the fuck your cousin tells you to and for heaven's sake none of your bullshit, you pull any shit Mouth and I swear it's gonna be your ass."

"See what I mean, never a sweet word, you're such a sweetheart, I can't tell you what a pleasure it is looking forward to spending the rest of my life with you."

This fucking girl.

"Mouth, now's not the time, somebody made a play for you, don't you get that?"

"Shane, how much do you know about my father and his organization? Somebody's always making a play for me; I'm the hottest bargaining chip in the underworld. Why do you think I do what I do?"

My stomach hurt hearing that shit, I never considered it like that, she was too fucking young to be dealing with that shit.

"Baby..." Fuck. "We'll talk when I get there, I'll see you soon, I love you."

I hung up the phone on her gasp.

Shit, did I just say that, I hadn't meant to, she just drew it out of me with her nonchalant way of describing her life as the daughter of the head honcho in the mob world. Yes it was easy to believe that she would've been the pampered, protected princess in her gilded cage, but there was the other side to that, the one where her father's enemies would try to use her to bring him down. Fuck, no wonder she was so tough; I'm such a dick for not putting it together sooner.

I still didn't want her involved in this shit, now more than ever I needed to go legit; I had to make her life safer. Before it was just something I wanted to do, I didn't want to play the heavy for the rest of my life like poppy, now it was about my family, me and Mouth and whatever kids we might have.

"Head to the estate guys."

Damn this shit was making me tired.

We pulled into the driveway of my parents' home, there were way more cars there than I expected, Mikey and Tony were as pissed as I was, after all their wives were involved too, and who knows what kind of shape ma was in. Shit, dad was not going to be too pleased with this shit.

I jumped out of the car before it came to a stop and went looking for her. There were lots of voices coming from inside as the boys came in behind me, hot on my heels.

They'd heard bits and pieces from my conversation with Tommy on the phone as well as the little bit I'd filled them in on; as much fun as we had picking on each other, these guys were serious as fuck when it came down to it, you fuck with their wives they'd go mental on a motherfucker, I might end up having to rein them in.

I bypassed everyone else, which included her father and uncle, and even Poppy, I don't want to know, I'll get to the bottom of that mess later, right now I needed to see my baby, make sure she was in one piece.

I should've known the nut would be fine, she was in the kitchen with ma and the girls, ma was sitting with a cup of tea, the cook Gerty was bustling around the kitchen throwing out orders as usual, the girls were regaling her with their latest adventure, and Arianna was looking through a magazine.

"Hey." I got halfway to her before the magazine came flying at my head.

"What the fuck?"

"Shane!"

"Ma..."

"You jerk..."

"What did I do now? Is it the price of gas...a new war broke out somewhere, one of your handbags went up another couple thousand, what?"

I kept going towards her, it had escaped my notice that everyone else had gone quiet; I was focused entirely on her. It didn't matter to me what the hell crazy notion she was on this time, she was whole, and she was fine. She was pissed.

"You tell me you love me for the first time over the phone?"

"What?"

I pulled her from the chair and into my arms before kissing the breath out of her.

"Oh Shane, how could you?"

"Ma, why are you always siding with Mouth? I thought I was your darling son here?"

The girls snickered just as Mikey and Tony came to see about them, hopefully they'd drag them off somewhere so they could stay the hell outta my business. I should've known better.

"You are my darling son, but you're also a man, tsk, tsk, tsk, and after all my hard work."

"What, you tried to turn me into a girl or some shit?" I was confused.

"No dear, but I did try to instill some sense into you, you know, so things like this didn't happen. All those lessons down the drain, you're locking your future wife away in closets, threatening her with all manner of things and now this. No candlelight Shane, not even a flower?" She shook her head like I was an imbecile.

"Ma, Mouth doesn't need that shit..."

"And her name is Arianna."

Mouth poked her tongue out at me. Cute.

"Ma I love ya, but you have no idea what's going on here trust me, as for me telling her I love her over the phone at least I said it, that should be good enough."

"That's right Casanova, you tell them." Mouth snarked at me, she even had the nerve to roll her eyes at me after saying that shit, like she'd been professing her undying love for me or some shit. I'm so not having this fucking conversation right now; can you imagine the two nightingales? Shit.

"Forget this shit, is somebody going to tell me what the hell happened?"

She elbowed me in the gut and then gave a slight shake of the head before indicating ma.

Oh I get it; we're pretending everything was okay for ma's sake.

"What the hell is she doing here?"

"Hey look it's Jimmy, how the hell is it sitting Jimmy bean?"

Fuck me, I forgot about him, the two jackasses started laughing, ma wanted to know how Ari knew her James and my sisters were looking back and forth between them with a quizzical look. It only took Poppy and the two old murdering bastards to join the fray to round out the circus, looks like dad wasn't here yet.

"Hey junior, no love for your Pop Pop? Quite a looker you got there, and I hear she's nifty with a bow and arrow." He howled with laugher like that shit was funny.

Kill me, kill me now.

Chapter 4

The kitchen was a fucking madhouse; Mouth and Jimmy as she torturously kept calling him, were taking swipes at each other. Poppy, Rossi and Alphonso were up to no fucking good how do I know, they were breathing weren't they? Murdering fucks.

Mom was in her glory having all these people to take care of, and the two jackasses and my sisters were making googly eyes at each other.

Outside the house must look like the president was in residence, the amount of manpower surrounding the place was out of fucking control but no way was I gonna take any chances with her safety.

By tactful agreement no one was mentioning what had happened at the mall. All I gathered so far in the few rushed minutes I'd stolen with Tommy was that Mouth recognized some fuck named Joey three fingers or some shit, she'd made him, he'd drawn his piece and she'd somehow outmaneuvered him and alerted Tommy and they'd gotten ma and the girls out of there instead of going after the guy.

What I wanted to know was why were they coming after her? If the faction that had been after Rossi was dead, then why the fuck were people coming after her here?

This fingers guy was supposedly a free agent so no one knew for sure who the fuck he was working for at least that's what Tommy thought; I'll have to look into it.

Rumor has it that he never missed, there's always a first time for everything and he'd missed today which meant to keep his reputation he was going to have to make another play.

I'm getting tired of people fucking with what's mine.

Fucking mob was like a three-headed snake, you cut one of those fuckers off and another one took its place.

"You're marrying her?"

I came back to the here and now at James's outburst.

"What the fuck, who are you talking to?" He knew better than to question me like that, ma or not I'd fuck his shit up right here I'd had enough.

"Uhm...." He looked like he'd swallowed something sour or some shit, like he was about to crap himself.

"Sorry."

"Don't fuck with me James."

"I still don't understand how Arianna knows our James, he hasn't been out of the house in quite sometime not since his accident I don't think.

"They met when I sent him on an errand ma that's all."

"Hey Ari is this the one you capped?"

Alphonso the fuck had to open his big mouth.

"What?"

"Nothing ma, he's kidding."

She didn't say anything else but she was looking all kinds of skeptical.

I gave the Rossi brothers a shut the fuck up look but they just smirked at me. The fucks. I wonder which one Mouth got the attitude problem from?

As soon as it was possible we men excused ourselves to the study, dad was still at the hospital but he wouldn't have had much to do with the meeting anyway, then again with mom involved he might've wanted in.

"Okay, so who's this Joey fingers what the fuck?" I got right to the point, no sense in beating around the bush.

"He's a wildcard, the best iceman in Chicago." Alphonso lit a cigar as he pulled up a seat.

"Word is he never misses." That's what I was most concerned about, the fact that these guys never quit.

"Nope, not once in twenty years. Rossi answered.

"He missed today, which means he'll be back."

"That's my kid, we did good there Alphonso.

"Damn straight, she would've made an excellent Don."

"Fuck that noise, she's not running your outfit, we're getting married and she's staying here with me."

There was a look passed between the two old fucks, Poppy meanwhile hadn't said a word, but the look on his face said it all. He was enjoying the show.

"What, what the fuck's that look about?"

"I'm guessing she hasn't told you that she's planning to return to Chicago in a few days."

I heard her father as if from a distance, fuck me not this shit again. I jumped up and flung the door to the study open.

"Arianna get over here now."

She came from the living room where the women had congregated.

"You bellowed your crankiness?"

I pulled her into the room and slammed the door shut.

"You're not going to Chicago."

"What?" She glared at her father and uncle.

"Don't look at them look at me, tell me you understand what I just said, you are not going to Chicago, no way no how."

"It's only for a short while."

"No."

"Shane..."

I cut her off with a hand around her throat.

"Mouth do not fuck with me on this, you only think you've seen me pissed, push me on this and live to regret it."

Mikey and Tony came to flank me, but funnily enough her father and uncle did nothing; not that I'd really hurt her but I did have my hand wrapped around her throat about to throttle her.

"Shane maybe you should..."

"Stay out of it Anthony she wants to pull the tiger's tail, let her see what happens.

"Son it's only for a short time, she has some unfinished business, there's still some cousins or some shit left from the family that was in bed with the Staccos, she asked me if she could take care of it and I said yes."

"She's not going after any more fucking mobsters and especially not with my kid inside her."

You could hear a pin drop it got so deathly quiet then.

"Kid, what kid?" Rossi looked between us trying to make sense of my words.

"Your grandkid."

"Shane cut it out, dad don't listen."

Of course the room erupted in chaos with everyone speaking at once. I just stood back and watched, waiting to see where the chips would fall, no matter what though she wasn't going.

I grabbed the back of her shirt when she was about to lay into her uncle, she turned her furious glare on me but I didn't give two shits.

"See what you started, are you happy now?"

"Tone it down Mouth, I'm not sure exactly why you think I handed you my balls but I've got news for you, don't fucking push me, and when exactly were you planning on telling me about this imaginary trip of yours? Or were you planning on skipping out without telling me?"

"Of course I was going to tell you, I was just waiting for the right moment." She turned her glare back on her father and uncle. No wonder she thought I should be afraid of her; both men seemed to cower under her scrutiny. Big fucking chance of that happening.

"It's a moot point now anyway, you're not going and Mouth believe me, if you should by some miracle get away and head there, I promise you you will wish you'd never met the likes of me."

"Don't threaten me Joe Scarponi."

"It's not a threat."

I saw her gulp when she got a good look at my face. Good, maybe now she'd take me seriously, because the last time she disobeyed me was the last time she disobeyed me.

"I don't see why..."

"Get this Arianna, there's no discussion, you're not going to fucking Chicago or anywhere else. These fucks found you here somehow; did you stop to think of that? You're being hunted like fucking prey. Kid or no kid I would've never let you go. You wanna sulk, fucking sulk, you want to throw a tantrum do that shit too but you'll be doing it here."

I pulled her into my body and lifted her chin so she could see into my eyes.

"I love you, but you'll never run me, the sooner you learn that the better off we'll be."

I took my phone from my jacket pocket and placed a call.

"Get me the twins."

"Oh shit." Michael shook his head and looked at Arianna with pity.

"Who're the twins?" she looked from Tony to Mikey who just shook their heads at her.

Chapter 5

"What did I tell you Rossi? match made in heaven." Poppy laughed his ass off.

What the fuck!

"Poppy what do you mean?" I looked from one to the other of the three old mobsters in my father's study, what the fuck was going on here, did they...?

"Poppy what the fuck is going on?"

"Who're the twins mob boy?"

"Not now Mouth, just know that your days of running wild are over; I have shit to take care of in the next few months so I can't be there every second of every day to ride herd on your stubborn ass so deal with what's coming."

If looks could kill I'd be dead, she better keep her little ass quiet or it'll be worst. Fuck, we weren't even married yet and already she was driving my ass nuts.

I turned back to my wily grandfather and his cohorts, they were busy whispering and gesticulating, probably arguing about how much to tell me.

From Poppy's little bombshell I gathered they think they have something to do with Mouth and I meeting.

"Start talking you three."

They came to a standstill in their little brouhaha as all eyes turned to them.

Alphonso and Rossi looked sheepishly at Mouth, while Poppy the old fuck could care less.

He looked me dead in the eye as he started.

"Listen up boyo, you weren't doing anything about carrying on the family name, I'm old and two steps out of the grave I want to bounce my great grandbabies on my knees for fucks sakes.

"What the fuck?"

"What about me Poppy?"

"James boy you know I love you but I've always been honest with you and I'm not about to stop now. You're not of my blood, doesn't mean I love you any less but I'm an old Irishman, blood will tell."

James looked like he was about to fucking break into tears.

"Poppy, that's fucked up, I get what you're saying but it's still fucked."

I wouldn't say anymore because I knew Poppy would stick to his guns, James will just have to handle his shit. I have bigger fish to fry right now anyway I'll deal with my brother's emotional trauma later.

"So you decided that I needed to be put out to stud?" Did I mention I was getting pissed way the fuck off?

"No, no, don't look at it like that, we were just trying a little matchmaking, it's something her father and I came up with years ago before you were even born, hell your own father wasn't even born yet when we made the deal.

Rossi looked nervous as fuck and Alphonso for some strange reason was silent and seemed to be trying valiantly to disappear into the wall.

"Dad..."

"Don't start Ari, you fell in love didn't you?"

She sniffed her nose at me, I still had a hold of her shirt, I'd forgotten that. I moved my hand around her waist and pulled her under my arm.

"Whether I did or not you had no right to interfere."

"Of course I did, you're my only kid, did you think I was going to leave something as important as this up to chance?

I had to make sure your husband was strong enough to deal with your...quirkiness."

Quirkiness my ass, she's nuts plain and simple, but she's my nut now. I guess I can't be too mad at the meddling old biddies, they did somehow manage to orchestrate the best fucking thing to ever happen to me.

"Uncle Al....."

"What?" He tried to look innocent as he cleaned imaginary lint from his jacket sleeve.

"Wait until I tell auntie on you two."

"Oh shit girl, that's hitting way below the belt, you won't do that to your old uncle now would you?"

What a sap, the guy was really afraid of the women in his family.

"Who's auntie?" I squeezed Mouth to get an answer out of her, seems she wasn't talking to me.

"She's sort of our surrogate sister, use to have designs on Phonso when we were kids but he's playing hard to get."

"Fuck off Roberto." I can't believe the sap was actually blushing, whatever, back to the matter at hand; their meddling asses.

"There's no way you three could've orchestrated everything that transpired here."

"Not the crazy shit no, we just needed to get her into the city under your nose. Your grandfather knows you very well, he knew if he maneuvered it so you could find out what the owner of the pub was up to you'd take action there. He was actually supposed to be here looking after her but shit went wonky and there was a change of plans. Things still worked out fine though don't you think? She was here a good month or so before you knew she was here, we had to step things up, but after that you crazy kids did everything else on your own."

I gave this some thought, I had to admit they were pretty fucking slick and like

I said, I couldn't really be mad at them, but I had a feeling they weren't done.

"So you got us together, now what?"

"You're just going to let them get away with it?"

My bloodthirsty mafia girl wanted somebody's throat between her teeth.

"Leave it Mouth, no harm done.

There was a lot of throat clearing, James was still sulking and the Bobsie twins were quiet for once, probably sucking up every word to retell to their wives and laugh at me later.

I gave them the finger with just a look; they got the message, trying to look all cool and shit, fucking yentas.

I finally took a seat pulling Mouth down on my lap as I waited to hear what fuckery they had in store for me next.

"Here's the thing." Rossi once again took the lead "You're trying to go legit, in fact you're well on your way to being that, but I'm roads ahead of you. I've been going straight behind the scenes for two years now that's why those assholes decided to band together, the fucks."

I felt her stiffen on my lap; apparently this was news to her as well.

"Anyway your biggest problem seems to be the law, as we all know, it is more profitable to be a criminal than to be a law abiding citizen. Your grandfather, Alphonso and I will take care of that no problem; us old dragons know how to handle dinosaurs. Some of the families back in Chicago weren't too happy with my decision to go legit, but some were on board; I gave up some of my old contacts to the more upstanding of our brothers and told the others to go fuck themselves.

There're still two families left who are a thorn in my side, it's one of these two that sent that fucking gumbah after my kid I'm sure. We take out these two fucks and it's smooth sailing." He stopped to take a sip of water, so far so good.

"Okay, what else? You're cleaning up your end of things I'm cleaning mine, this is a good thing but your business is in Chicago mine's here, Mouth isn't going back to Chicago to run your shit, legal or otherwise so what was the point?"

"You'll run them both together."

The fuck! okay, that was some serious shit he was saying here. Rossi's organization made mine look like kids play, he controlled more than five times what I did.

"You'll have fifty five percent interest in the business, Ari gets the rest, plus you have your own business here."

"That's a very sweet deal, tell me, why would you do that for someone you just met and hardly know?"

"Boy I've been studying you for the past two years, even before your Poppy sold me on the idea, you see I got started later in life but the deal was my kid would marry his kid; since he got started way ahead of me I figured it was dead but then I started hearing good things about young Shane Flanagan so I started tracking you. When I called your Poppy a few months ago asking for help stashing Ari, he brought up the idea of a match between you two."

"Two years, when she was seventeen?"

"Boy that girl was born old, besides we thought we'd wait until she was eighteen, it's one year later but what the hell?"

The ball of fire was about to explode on my lap but there was a knock at the door. Michael got up to answer and the two men walked in.

"Hello boys." I stood with Mouth next to me. " Meet your new assignment."

"Boss...."

They both spoke at the same time with pained looks on their faces.

"I see you've heard the stories already."

They nodded their heads in unison.

"I'm sure you boys can handle it, didn't they teach you how to handle explosive weapons of mass destruction in the Seals?"

"Boss, uhm yeah, but she's yours."

"So you handle her with care in all things, if the situation warrants it I give you permission to use force."

I got an elbow to the gut as Mouth finally caught on to who the two new men in the room were.

The twins were anything but, Zane was a six foot four African American and Alec was a six foot six Native American, they got their nickname because of the way they moved together, like fucking magnets. It was from their days in the seals together.

"Arianna meet your two new best friends."

"I think I liked it better when you called me Mouth, every time you call me Arianna it's followed by bad news. No offense boys."

She smirked at the two men who were sizing her up. Probably wondering how someone so tiny could've pulled off all the shit they'd heard about. They'll learn.

Chapter 6

The Assassin

I heard the big boss man giving out his orders, he didn't know I was listening, sniggers, what he doesn't know won't hurt him.

He thought I was tucked away nice and comfy in bed. Of course he'd done his best to see to that, but as amazing as the sex was, he hadn't quite achieve his goal of knocking me out.

I was waiting to hear my name called, to see what he expected them to do where I'm concerned, but he was playing it safe.

He'd obviously called them as soon as he left the room and since they were now stationed on the same floor in a room set up no doubt to spy on me, I needed all the info I could get.

I was enjoying their frustration as to what was the best course of action though I did take offense to being called a little rascal, until he mentioned his ex skank, and what he had to say made me see red.

Now I've been ignoring that bitch all this time, all the snide remarks and bitchy looks and all the other bullshit she pulled when I was at the club. I'd let it all slide, after all it wasn't my place...then, but since Don Umberto thinks he owns me, threatens me with his kid and all manner of things, what's his is mine.

Plus the three old meddling ya yas decided to sell us out, building their own little empire on our backs, so to speak. Sheeeeiiiiiit, we're a team made in mafia hell.

That said, mob boy can't get mad at me for what I'm about to do, we're partners after all.

Right?

Prince of The City

"She's gone."

"What?"

"Arianna, she's not in the apartment."

"How do you know, you didn't even leave the room."

"I just know, we're like connected or some shit.

I pulled out my phone to call her other detail out on the street, she'd fooled me once, not gonna happen again plus I knew her hardheaded ass wouldn't stay still for too long.

I'd known she was feigning sleep when I left her well fucked ass in my bed, what I didn't know is where the hell she was off to now.

"You got her?"

"Yeah, right on her, I don't think she made us... yet, if she does what do we do?"

"Nothing, you stay on her until she's back here. Where's she off to anyway?"

"It looks like she's heading to the club, she's walking kind of fast, looks kinda pissed."

"I'm heading out, keep her in your sights at all times, you guys got the picture of this Joey fingers fuck right so be on the lookout for him.

I hung up with them and turned to Alec and Zane.

"Let's go round up my little hellion, I doubt she's going to the club to work so Lord knows what she's up to."

They looked like they were fighting laughter, fuck, I'm surrounded by comedians, first the two sisters in law, now these two.

My phone beeped just as we jumped into my car.

My boy Dominic calling me with the news that Mouth had indeed entered the club; I was only about three minutes behind her.

I didn't see her anywhere on the floor and no one mentioned her as I exchanged greetings with the staff as I passed them.

I didn't bother asking anyone if they'd seen her, If she'd wanted to be recognized they would've noticed her entrance, not knowing why she was here I thought it prudent to keep her presence a secret just in case.

Alec and Zane brought up the rear as we headed towards the offices in the back.

We heard her before we saw her.

I held my hand up for them to stop and wait; we crept forward towards the door of Ricci's office that was slightly cracked open giving us enough room to see the two women inside.

"So what was your plan skank, get me out of the way so you can have him, how stupid can you be, if he'd wanted your psychotic ass he would be with you, not me."

Damn my baby was being all female, didn't know she had it in her. So that's what she was doing, I'll have to be more careful in the future if I had something I wanted kept from her, like drugging her ass to sleep so I could have a conversation in peace. Little sneak.

"Well if you hadn't shown up and thrown yourself at him we would be together now."

"Do you even hear yourself, what kind of fucked up shit are you on, seriously if he loved you it wouldn't matter who came on the scene he'd still be with you, besides didn't he drop your ass long before I came along?"

"That was just temporary..."

"What the fuck ever Alex Forrest."

"Who?" Ricci looked lost as fuck, that'll happen if you got caught up in conversation with the mouthy one.

"You ever seen Fatal Attraction?"

"You're so juvenile, I don't know what he could possibly see in you, in fact I bet if your father wasn't some big time mobster he'd never have given you the time of day."

She clapped her hand over her mouth as if to pull the words back in.

Too late.

"How did you know that? No one here knows about that so how do you?"

"I don't know what you're talking about of course everyone knows I must've heard it from one of the others.

"No you didn't, who've you been talking to about me what else you've been up to? That James guy is an easy mark for a tramp like you, who else did you trap with your funky coochie?"

"How dare you, you little bitch."

"We can't all be Amazons lurch; now back to how you knew about my dad."

Teresa suddenly was all smiles, like she knew something that no one else did. I didn't like that shit.

"We found it out James and I, we also found out that your old man is dead and you're his heir but there are some who want you dead. So I placed some calls and let it slip, anonymously of course, that you're here, but it looks like I didn't need their fancy hit man after all, I'll get to do you in myself and collect the money anyway, nice bonus."

She pulled a silver semiautomatic glock from her drawer and pointed it at Mouth.

What the fuck?

I moved quickly into the room but Mouth was faster.

She moved so fast it was like a blur, her hands and feet in constant motion, when it was all said and done Teresa laid on the floor with a broken neck, the gun was in Mouth's hand and I still didn't know what had happened. Fuck me I'm so screwed.

My crazy fucking fiancé looked down at the no longer breathing woman on the floor and said "Oh by the way, you're fired."

"Fuck boss where did you find her, Moussad?"

"What?" I turned to Alec and Zane who I'd somehow forgotten was there, I was still trying to get my breathing back under control and my heart to go the fuck back where it belonged. This girl was going to be the death of me no joke.

"That's Krav Maga, I think we need to renegotiate boss, how long did you say you needed us on her?"

"Oops."

This from the nut who just realized that she had company.

"Oops? Oops? That's it mouth, for fucks sake you just took ten years off my fucking life. I'm locking your ass away somewhere, somebody somewhere must've made something that can keep your ass secured"

Chapter 7

The Assassin

At first I thought he was just pissed and I was about to let him have it, until I saw the real fear in his eyes, he was terrified.

"I was never in any danger Shane."

I ran my hand up and down his back soothingly; I could feel the pounding of his heart through his jacket.

Fuck, I'd really scared him.

"Take care of that."

He ordered his team before dragging me out of the room.

We took the emergency exit out the back and he had his phone to his ear as we went around the side of the building.

"Any sign of this fuck yet?"

I guess that was a negative because he hung up the phone with a furtive 'fuck'.

I was gently placed in the front seat of the car he had waiting, my seat belt buckled for me before he climbed into the driver's side.

All this was done with not one word to me, I kept watching him out the side if my eye as we drove through the empty streets.

We drove into the underground garage; I was once again helped out of the car, all the way up in the elevator he kept his hand in the small of my back but he didn't look at me and didn't speak.

"Shane..."

"Ssh...."

He kissed me then like I was his last link to life, like he needed me more than air, it was a toe curling, and heart consuming kiss and it scared the crap out of me.

He was not acting the way I expected him to.

Back in the apartment he walked straight to the en suite bathroom and ran a bath.

I sat on the side of the bed confounded. What the hell was going on?

He undressed me and led me into the bathroom, still not a sound.

Helping me into the tub, he got undressed and climbed in behind me, drawing me back against his chest.

His hands came under my arms to rest on my stomach and with a deep sigh, he laid his head back.

My Body stayed stiff for all of two minutes more before I relaxed.

As we got ready for bed, still in total silence I kept calling his name, he kept kissing me into silence.

In bed he drew my body under his, his lips traveling from my neck down to my nipple, where he licked and sucked me until it was rock hard before moving onto the other one.

His large hand made its way down between my thighs, two big fingers moving in and out of me as he made love to my breasts with his mouth.

Lifting his head he took my lips in a kiss as his fingers quickened their pace inside me. When I came, it was long and soft and sweet.

When he climbed on top of me and entered me with our eyes held, it was beautiful magic.

"I love you Arianna."

"I love you too Shane."

Our bodies moved together in perfect sync, his hands on my body bringing me to fever pitch, his softly whispered words of love going straight to my heart.

"There's no one more beautiful or more desirable than you, there never will be."

"Oh..." I felt myself tighten around him.

"I'm going to love you forever beautiful. Will you marry me?"

He took my finger and the ring into his mouth and bit down as he thrust faster into me. I had to wait until I could breathe again before I could give him my answer.

"Yes...yes I'll marry you."

Prince of The City

"You're an assassin aren't you?"

It was morning; I had laid awake half the night thinking about what I'd seen. The guys had called in to report that Ricci's body had been disposed of.

We'd had someone pretending to be Teresa call upstairs to say she wasn't feeling well and that I was sending a replacement, I had one of my other managers go in to finish out the shift.

No one was any the wiser, after a few days I'd plant the rumors that she left because of my engagement to Mouth I'm sure it wouldn't be too hard to believe.

Now here we are still in bed, still wrapped around each other and I have no idea how to deal with this shit.

There's no way you can cloister that shit, it's inside of her, I saw it with my own fucking eyes. No matter how much she claims she never wanted to be a part of this life, it was as much a part of her, as it was I.

"Are you.........an assassin?"

She looked at me for a long time until tears formed in her eyes and rolled down her cheeks.

"Dad thought I should know all the ways to protect myself, there was always someone after us so from the age of five I've been trained in most hand-to-hand combat starting with Tae kwon do. I know most of the Eastern arts, I can dismantle and put a gun back together in under a minute and a half but I'm still working on that.

My specialty is the bow and arrow; I started taking archery classes when I was about eight or nine.

My first kill was at fifteen; one of dad's enemies sent one of his goons after me. He tried to get me at school. I broke his neck with my bare hands then got sick all over him, dad and uncle Al came as soon as I called them with the cleaner.

They took me home and took care of me until my aunt Charlotte got there then she took over. We never talked about it, only at night when the nightmares chased me from sleep; dad would hold me and rock me until I calmed down again.

After that I made a promise, I'd only kill to protect myself or my own, I don't like it Shane, I hate it, every time I've done it I've lost a part of myself, but there's something inside me that whenever one of my loved ones are in danger, I go into this other place in my head.

I lost my mom I won't lose anyone else I won't lose you."

She hugged me tightly as I put together the words she'd said. Fucking killing machine, what the fuck?

I wonder if she realized she'd just described a stone cold killer? The zone she was trying to describe, that place she went to in her head, the kill zone.

And it was my job to tame that shit, fuck my life, I'd rather take on the fucks who were out to get me than try to keep this one chained.

Fucking Mouth, she looked so fucking innocent too, the girl barely reached my chin, but what I'd seen last night, fuck, if I wasn't getting out of the business I'd hire her. I wasn't telling her that shit though she was a handful already no sense in encouraging her murdering ass.

I wonder if Poppy knew about her special talents? I wouldn't put it past him, with her being a silent killer and me being the fuck the morherfuckers type, they had a match made in mafia heaven.

One thing was for damn sure, I had to hurry up and get my shit together before mouth killed off half the fucking city.

Chapter 8

"Where does it end Arianna?"

"What do you mean?"

"When will you have killed all your enemies, how many others are there?"

"That's not fair."

"It's a legitimate question, obviously you don't care how I feel about it so I'd like to know if this is going to be a lifetime thing, or will you get tired of it soon?"

"Shane why are you talking this way, I thought you'd understand... I thought..."

"What's the point of me going legit if you're going around being a killing machine? Maybe we should both just say fuck it and carry on as before.

We'd kill everyone who opposes us, take over the whole Western faction and parts of the Midwest, why stop now..."

"Shane stop it, that's not what I'm doing..."

"Let me ask you something, what do you think love is?"

"What...what do you mean?"

"If you love someone do you want the best for them or the worst?"

"The best of course."

"Do you think it's best that you be a part of this, something that you admit chips away at your very soul? I know how that feels Arianna, I live it, do you honestly think I could want that for you?"

Do you think I object to you doing this because you're a woman? No baby, I didn't want this for my little brother after I got into the life either, for all that he's a fuck up.

I always thought I wanted to be in the life, I wanted to be like Poppy, I thought it made me tough, a real man, but that's not true. I could be a janitor and still be a real man.

I had two extremes in my life as examples, my dad would lay down his life to save another, he believes strongly in preserving life, Poppy, Poppy was from another time, another belief.

It wasn't always killings and gang wars; it used to be about family, that's long gone now.

"Regardless of all that, I've come to a decision."

I felt her stiffen against me, she probably expected me to give her an ultimatum, but I was beyond that, this was way more serious than I'd ever imagined.

The woman I had given my heart to was more than just the mouthy baggage I'd come to know, there was a whole lot more to her than that, but what I knew was that she did not choose this life, it had been forced on her by necessity, she was still carrying this torch because she thought she had to.

I was about to make a play that could blow up in my face, but there was no way we could go on like this, I couldn't live with it, it just wasn't in me.

"You're done..."

"What?"

I pushed her head back down on my chest.

"You're done, I'll take over whatever you have to finish in Chicago, I know your strength, I've seen it, I know you're not weak, I respect your strength, be strong enough to stand down Arianna, this became my fight when you became mine, my woman, my responsibility.

Don't make me have to waste time fighting you and our enemies at the same time, you won't win, you've come to the end of the road.

You've been testing me all this time and I didn't even see it, you wanted to see if I could take care of you, that might not be your exact thinking, but you can't deny you've been testing me, your father and uncle missed that step, they didn't see the little girl who just wanted normal, they applauded your achievements without realizing that you were just doing what you thought was expected, well now I'm telling you, you don't have to do that shit anymore because I've got you.

It's my place to protect you and whatever children we might have, don't get me wrong, I'm proud as fuck that you can handle yourself, but I don't ever want you to have to, so I'm asking you, pass the torch Arianna, let me finish this fight, you're free."

She didn't say anything for so long that I thought she had gone to sleep, I wouldn't put it past her, but then I felt the wetness against my chest.

"Mouth?"

I tried raising her head to see if she was actually crying but she held on tighter until I felt the slight tremors in her body.

I wrapped both arms around her drawing her in tighter, turning to my side with her held tightly in my arms, I let her cry it out.

Chapter 9

"You can't tell dad and uncle Al." She laid with her head on my chest.

"Never." I rubbed my hands soothingly over her, kissing her hair, my poor baby.

"They'll feel guilty and I don't want that."

"It's okay baby." I dried her tears with my fingertips.

"I love all of you always, everything you are baby."

She was through crying thank heaven, I can't stand that shit, it drives me crazy.

She'd just revealed herself to me, told me all her secrets and in doing so she'd shown me so much more. She'd shown me that she needed as far away from this shit as possible, which meant I had to step up my game.

Her whole youth had been taken up with this bullshit; she should never have felt like she had to be a killing machine in order to survive.

I can't imagine Anna or Sophie living that way, I wanted her to have what the women in my family had, pampering and frivolity, days of shopping and long lunches with friends not a care in the fucking world other than where was the next big sale.

Getting her hair and nails done just because, all the things the girls and ma took for granted, I would see that she got that, all of it.

That was for later though, right now I needed her, needed to feel her warmth wrapped around me, to reassure myself that she was here and whole and mine.

We started with slow kisses and soft touches as I murmured words of love and admiration in her ear; I felt the need to show her just how much she was loved, how much she touched me, what she meant to me.

With her ring hand clasped in mine, our eyes connected, I eased into her until she had all of me.

"My sweet, sexy, little warrior princess."

She liked that, if the tightening around my cock was any indication.

"Kiss me...." I teased her with small strokes as she fought to pull me all the way in again.

She raised her head until her lips touched mine, divine.

That shit went right through me, proving to me once more just how completely I was gone, so gone that she could own me with a kiss.

Her soft hands clutched at my back as I rocked into her, somehow the sight of that ring, my seal of ownership on her finger, made this so much more, like everything was intensified.

I wanted to give her soft and sweet, she needed that, but my body begged me for more.

Animal.

I gritted my teeth to hold back the demands of my wayward libido, even as I pulled out of her and clamped my mouth over her heated sex.

She lifted her hips, taking more of my tongue into her as her fingers tugged my hair. My dick was oozing pre cum all over the sheets as I rubbed myself against them. I needed to calm the fuck down before I hurt her.

Where this wildness came from out of nowhere was a mystery, but it was here and it won't be denied.

I needed to fuck, to claim, to overpower, it was like a beating in my blood.

I forced her to orgasm with my tongue before getting to my knees and turning her none too gently onto her hands and knees.

I pounded into her making her whole body shake, she screamed and looked back at me, eyes wide in surprise.

I'd never quite fucked Mouth like a wild animal before; she'd brought this out of me, this need to take my place as man, to own her in all ways. I needed to conquer.

"Take it..."

She grabbed ahold of the rumpled sheets as I battered her pussy from behind, with my hand on her neck keeping her head down in the mattress, her ass in the air, her pussy stuffed full of my cock she was exactly where I wanted her. In submission.

"Shane...what...oh merciful..."

I used more force in my thrusts as her hips pushed back against me, she was wet and hot and so fucking good.

"Cum...." I commanded her.

Moving my hand, I bit into her neck as I flooded her insides with cum, causing a chain reaction in her.

We came calling for each other.

My life was one of peace for all of two hours, maybe, what made me think this shit would be any different was beyond me.

No sooner had I left the apartment to go get started on what the fuck I had to do than the twins were calling me to tell me what she was up to.

What part of stay your little ass in the house until we catch this finger fuck guy she didn't understand I don't know.

I picked up the phone to call her.

"Where were you off to sneak?"

"My apartment, I need to get some of my things, in case you haven't noticed since you dragged me off to your cave I haven't been back to get my necessities."

"You had a chance to do that and you used it to sneak out and go work at the club, or did you forget that?"

"That was then, this is now...

I hung up the phone, she'd argue me to death otherwise, I was satisfied that the men could keep her in check while I saw to things, they'd assured me that they knew her fighting style now and that they'd just been surprised when they'd seen her in action, but they were satisfied that they could handle their shit.

I'm having a meeting with the three murdering bastards, as I'd grown fond of calling them, it was time to put this shit to bed.

I'm giving mouth one more week before dragging her ass to the doctor to confirm her pregnancy, I hope to heaven that she is and that it keeps her little ass out of trouble.

Why couldn't I have fallen for a sweet little even-tempered girl whose only thought in life was pleasing me?

Even I had to laugh at that shit, I'd shoot myself in the fucking head within a week. With my mouthy one there was sure to be enough excitement to keep me going for at least the next sixty years.

If she let me live that long, she was going to be pissed when she found out what I had planned.

Too fucking bad, I wasn't playing when I said she was done, I knew her game now, if she needed me to prove to her that I was man enough to protect her then I'll just have to show her.

She was going to be a pampered spoilt wife if it killed me.

Chapter 10

I watched them as they walked into my office, three middle-aged men, well one a little older than that.

From their carriage and demeanor you'd swear they were the CEOs of some fortune 500 company, no one would ever guess that they built their empires on sweat and blood, literally.

You couldn't see the steel that held their backs up, just what they wanted the world to see. Men of means, men with purpose.

I have a lot of admiration and respect for each of these men, for what they've achieved by fair means or foul.

I'm the expected heir to their achievements, me and my soon to be wife and children.

It was good that they'd instigated change or else there would've been a rift as I was now at that place where I too wanted change.

I wanted to run an empire that I could be proud of, that my children could inherit without fear.

I'm not turning pussy, don't get that shit twisted, but I do want to spend the rest of my days as more of a businessman and less of a criminal.

I wanted that for Ari more than I wanted anything else, wanted her free of all this shit; I'll make that happen even if I have to knock some heads together.

"Come in and sit down gentlemen."

"Flanagan." Alphonso was the first one in.

"Hey boy." I wish her father would stop calling me that shit but it wasn't serious enough to warrant a confrontation.

"Junior." Poppy had a smarmy smile on his face as usual; I wonder how many times he wore that same look even as he pulled the trigger?

"Gentlemen."

I looked at each of them in turn.

"First things first, before we do anything else I have a bone to pick with you two."

Larry and Moe pointed back and forth between each other before turning to me.

Shit, now she had me thinking in TV speak.

"What can we do for you young'un?"

Rossi sat forward and clasped his hands between his knees.

The glare in his eyes reminded you that he was a dangerous animal not to be fucked with, though the casual easiness of his body fooled you into thinking otherwise.

I didn't give a fuck.

"I know what you're up to, my guys uncovered your little scheme, now I've already told your little killing machine now I'm telling you, she's out, you fucks try going around me with this shit and you're fucked."

"Watch it junior, you don't want to be talking to grown men like that."

"Stuff it Poppy, I want you two to know I mean business, now I know you're afraid of her...."

"What, that's bullshit...."

"I watched you Alphonso, you too Rossi, I don't mean scared like a little bitch scared, but you're afraid of her retribution, I must admit she's a scary little nut but she's done, if you think you're afraid of her try me, Poppy you know I'll do it."

"Okay everybody calm down." Poppy tried to play peacemaker.

"What is it you think you know Flanagan?"

"I know that you plan to have your daughter go to Chicago to finish what you started, that there're specifically two families there that need terminating, they're being dealt with as we speak, you see, as much as I like to get my hands dirty I'm trying to show her by example, if she can't, then neither can I."

"She wanted to do it, it means something to her."

"I understand that but she's not doing it, for fuck's sake she's already iced two people in the last week, that I know of I should say, I shudder to think what the fuck she could get up to in Chicago, so no, like I said I've got men on it already."

"She ain't gonna be happy."

"Fuck Alphonso she'll get over it, what is it with you two and this kid, she's fucking nineteen years old, you're supposed to be hard asses and yet she runs you."

"It's not that boy, there are things going on here that you don't know about."

"I know, she told me everything and that's why I'm telling you, she's out, she's my responsibility now and I choose for her not to be involved in this shit any farther. You had your chance, you did things your way now I'll do them mine."

"You finding fault with the way I raised my kid?"

"Yes." The fuck! I don't back down for anyone, well maybe except for Mouth once in a while.

No one said anything for the longest time, and then the crazy fucks started laughing. What the fuck?

"Flanagan you called it, fucking a old man, the boy's just the right one to get our girl in line."

Rossi slapped Poppy on the back while the three of them started congratulating one another like they'd single-handedly mastermind mine and Ari's relationship.

I wonder what they would've done if her mouth had caused me to pop her ass in the beginning?

"Moving right along, how's it going with those conniving fucks on the force?"

"That's not for you to worry about junior, we've already got some irons in the fire there, we just wanted to touch bases with you, let you know things are coming along, but I think you've thrown my friends here for a loop, didn't he boys?"

"Uh, you could say that." Rossi fixed his collar as he looked away from me. What now?

"What?"

"Well, you have to remember this is before you made your little announcement just now, we can't be held responsible for anything that happened before..."

"Spit it out old man."

"Well.... Ari was supposed to skip out and head back home to take care of things, we were kinda helping her with her escape."

I cleared my throat to give myself some time, it wouldn't do to choke the fuck out of my future father in law and 'Ari' would probably try to scalp me, but he sure was pushing it.

"Lucky for you and her my men would never let that happen."

Just then the phone rang.

The Assassin

"Shane you've got to get the Black knight and Eagle eyed Shaman off my ass."

"Deal with it." He hung up.

Did he just...oh hell no, I'm gonna go straight up honey boo boo on his ass.

"Shane said I could go."

I stared at my two new pains in the ass. Of course they didn't budge, didn't even bat a lash, shit.

I didn't exactly lie to Shane before, but I had to go, if I didn't it would be like an itch under my skin, something I had to get at until I was satisfied and the itching had abated.

I can't just turn off who I am just like that, he's acting as though I wanted to go around slaughtering innocent people or some shit, these guys tried to fuck my dad, It's not in me to let that shit slide, but this one had a burr up his butt and wanted to curtail my activities.

I bet he's off doing shit right now while I'm supposed to stay home like a good little lady and knit or some shit.

"Well didn't you hear me, he said it was fine."

The dark Knight unclipped some kind of phone from his belt and put it to his ear; I say some kind of phone because it didn't look like any phone I'd ever seen before.

"Yeah boss, Ms. Rossi says you said it was okay for her to go."

I rolled my eyes at him, tattletale.

He passed the device over to me, shit.

"Hello."

"Go." Click.

I looked at the phone, then at the two men standing in front of me and back again.

What just happened there? With one word, two letter's, he'd made me feel.... chastened.

What was I supposed to do with that?

"He said go." Was that my voice, it sounded hollow?

I almost broke when the two men stepped aside for me to pass, what did it mean?

I went over everything he'd said to me that morning and that night after I'd done Stacco.

I tried to realign my thinking with what he said but all I kept hearing was his dis-interested voice saying 'go'.

That hurt, why should it though, he was giving me what I asked for, what I wanted, wasn't he? Or was he playing me?

Chapter 11

I moved towards the door as if to leave, waiting for them to stop me…nothing, they weren't even watching me. I put my hand on the knob and turned it, opening it, I almost hoped to find armed guards out there blocking my path.

There was nothing, the hallway was empty, still; I came back into the room where the twins were lounging, looking through two magazines, they didn't say or do anything.

Well hell, what the hell was I supposed to do now?

I ran into the bedroom and got my phone, mob boy answered on the third ring.

"Hello."

"Shane?"

"Yes Arianna."

I didn't know what to say for the first minute so I just sat there with the phone glued to my ear.

"You told me to go."

He had the nerve to remain silent.

"Well say something."

"What is there to say?"

"Are you playing me?"

"No."

"So you don't care if I go?"

"You're a grown woman do as you please."

"That's it?" Silence again.

"Fine." I huffed into the phone.

He hung up again, what the fuck was going on here, was he mind fucking me or some shit?

My dad and uncle would never leave things like that, they'd have argued with me, though I'd still end up doing as I pleased, but still, they would've at least tried.

I didn't like this feeling one bit, listlessness, I didn't know whether to sit or stand, stay or go and my heart wasn't supposed to hurt like this, it never has.

I laid across the bed to give myself a break, maybe I'll take a nap, dealing with crazy guy had taxed my nerves, it felt like all my energy had deserted me. Needless to say I don't think I'll be going anywhere until we resolved this new issue of his dismissing me like a pesky little gnat.

Fucking guy.

Prince of The City

"Where is she?"

"I think she's laying down in the room, she's been in there for a good twenty minutes and we haven't heard a peep, but the monitor indicates she's not moving."

"Her trackers in place?"

"Yep."

"Any word on this fingers guy, what the fuck? How many three fingered guys we got walking around this shit anyway?"

"Honestly, I think the guy bounced, no one's seen him anywhere and you know your guys would've flushed him out by now. I seriously think he's running from her, I don't know if you've heard, but since you had our guys head to Chi Town there's been a lot of rumblings, seems your girl has a bit of a rep and the families that are going after her aren't just doing it because of her father, they think she'd be worst than he ever was, at least that's the word on the street there."

Yes, I know that's the word on the street in Chicago, that's why I'm being extra fucking careful to keep her ass here. No one's invincible and as good as she is, there's no guarantee she'd make it out alive. That's why I have to put an end to the ones who are after her before I do anything else. As far as telling her to go, I'm pretty sure she's won every argument she's ever had with the two men in her life, I'm not about to go down that path with her again, she doesn't need to know that I have no intentions of letting her go two feet outside the building, let her think I don't care, see what she does with that shit. Hardheaded fuck.

Two hours later she's still in the room, I wasn't worried, well not too much, but I remembered how she reacted the last time I told her we were quits and I had a pretty good idea what was going on with her. She'd crawled into her little protective shell, guess I'd just have to go drag her out again.

I left the office and headed home not knowing what madness was awaiting me there, with Mouth it could go either way, as long as she was there and in one piece I didn't give a fuck.

I made a quick stop on the way before continuing on, thank heaven I'd had the good sense to leave frick and frack in the car while I did my thing or these two asses would be getting on my nerves.

"I'm staying in for the rest of the day so you two girls can knock off, go get your nails done or some shit."

They each gave me the finger before laughing and pulling off.

Upstairs I dismissed the twins with the same offer, they were more circumspect in their replies, I got one fuck you and an up yours.

Mouth was asleep in our bed, she'd probably tired herself out coming up with ways to kill me off for messing with her, what was I gonna do with this girl? Every time I thought we'd squared shit she'd get another wild hair. I'm not sure what the fuck is the right course of action anymore but I did know what I wanted to be doing in the next five minutes.

Moving around the room quietly I had her pretty much where I wanted her by the time she began to stir.

I'd tied her arms and legs to the posts, not too tight because I didn't want to wake her, but now she was coming to I tightened her arms first and then her legs.

Before she could open her mouth to blast me I was on her, my mouth covering hers as I led my already throbbing cock into her heat.

"You..."

"Later..." I cut her off with a forceful thrust that lifted her off the bed. I didn't want to talk, not now; right now I just wanted to feel her; this new dominant streak she'd brought out in me needed to be appeased.

"I fucking missed being inside you all day, now I have you at my mercy, I think we'll stay like this for the rest of the afternoon, any objections?" I didn't give her time to answer as I plunged into her hard, rough, forcefully.

"Ahhhhhh...untie my hands, I want...I want to touch you too."

"No, I like you just like this, I can do anything I want to you and there's nothing you can do, like this...."

I pulled out and attached my mouth to her weeping cunt, she screamed and twisted under my onslaught, begging me to stop one minute and ordering me not to in the next.

Not to worry, I wasn't planning on stopping anytime soon, all day I'd been worrying about her running off to Chicago, the danger she would face there not to mention the fact that I would miss the fuck out of her was more than I could stand.

I ate her pussy until she flooded my mouth and chin, before driving back into her, pinning her beneath me as I bit and sucked on her neck and chest.

Her pussy felt better than ever before, the fact that I had her spread out beneath me and at my mercy made my dick hard as fuck as thoughts of all the things I wanted to do to her worked to make me rut her like a bull in a stall, I fucked her through two orgasms before cumming like a fucking geyser inside her.

"Fucking perfect."

I teased her with my lips before untying her from the bed, should've known she wouldn't let me win that easily.

I found myself on my back with her elbow across my throat, I put up no resistance, and fought really hard to keep my laughter in check, Lord knows what the nut would do to me in this position.

"Hello sweetheart." I thought my delivery was good but the Mouth rolled her eyes at me before snorting and gut punching me.

She rolled away from me before I could grab her.

"Come here Mouth."

"Why did you tell me to go? You just threw me away like I didn't matter to you."

Now I was the one rolling my eyes, if she thought I was going to fall for her shit again she was sorely mistaken and even if she wasn't putting me on, I'm still not playing into the her hands.

This one is going to keep me on my toes in more ways than one, my ideal of a contented housewife who loves nothing more than staying home with the kids was fast becoming a pipe dream, her little ass is just wired different.

I'm beginning to think being in the mob might be easier than taming this one but I'm going to give it my best damn shot.

I waited until she got close again and pulled her down beside me, it's amazing how just a few short months ago I had no knowledge of this girl, but right now my world would be fucked without her in it.

"You said you wanted to go, I was just being a good fiancé and giving you what you want."

I got another punch to the gut for my sarcasm.

"By the way I got you something."

I jumped off the bed and retrieved the package I'd dropped when I came in. Bringing it back to the bed I laid it across her chest.

"What's this?" She scoffed when she saw the home pregnancy test.

"The lady at the pharmacy said you can use this anytime of the day, go pee on the stick Mouth."

"I will not." She was back to being her pain n the ass self again, that didn't take long.

"What's the matter you scared? The big bad mob girl is afraid of a little baby, say it ain't so babe, say it ain't so."

She was off the bed and in the bathroom in the flash; I held my laughter until the door was closed or she'd probably do me physical harm.

With my hands behind my head I relaxed and waited.

When I thought of what was going on behind that door my body had a strange reaction. My dick got hard as fuck at the thought that even now she could be learning that she was carrying our first child. Shit.

"Hurry up in there Mouth." I was about to embarrass myself; one more minute and she'd exit that room to find me jerking my meat.

The need for her was powerfully strong all of a sudden; who knew the thought of fatherhood would be an aphrodisiac?

The empty box flying at my head should've been a total turnoff, but the fire breathing dragon that screeched at me, 'Flanagan you knocked me up you dick' was too delightful to resist.

It wasn't exactly hard tackling her to the bed, though she did put up a bit of a fight.

"Gotcha."

Chapter 12

"Flanagan I swear I will make you pay for this."

"Pay for what sweetheart, planting my seed, staking my claim, tying your ass down?" Maybe I should quit while I'm ahead, she wasn't looking too warm and fuzzy, in fact she looked like she wanted to do my ass in.

"So what're you saying, you don't want to have my kid?"

"Of course that's not what I'm saying, it's just that...quit gloating before I garrote you mob boy."

I held my hands up in surrender. "No gloating, see...." I tried to keep a straight face but I couldn't pull it off.

Fuck yeah I was gloating, are you kidding me? This kid was just what the doctor ordered, maybe now she'd keep her little ass where I put her, my life should be smooth sailing form here on out.

I poked her with my raging hard on and she resisted out of sheer stubbornness until I bit the underside of her jaw while rubbing my leaking cock head against her clit, then she opened up and let me in.

Somehow being inside her, knowing that my child was in there made me feel even more excited than usual. With her beautiful face caught in my hands, I smiled into her eyes as I moved in and out of her.

"I can't believe my little prince is in there right now."

"It's a girl." I just grinned at her contrariness, I could care less, boy or girl, I win.

"You going to listen to me now, huh, you going to be my good girl?"

She squeezed down on my dick to show me who was in charge. It worked too because when she started working those muscles every thought flew right out of my head.

I didn't put up much of a fight when she rolled us over and ended up on top, my hands held flat on the bed beneath hers as she rode my cock until my toes curled.

She added a new twist to her motion, her ass flexing back and forth as she took me over. She moved my hands and put them behind her, right on her gorgeous ass cheeks.

I dug in and gave as good as I got but I'm no fool, this was her show, I was tempted to believe that all her arguments were just for show, it sure seemed like finding out she had my bun in the oven made her wild if the way she rode my dick was any indication.

Using my hands on her ass I pounded up into her, hard, until I remembered.

"Shit, is this safe?"

"If you stop it won't be for you."

She actually growled that shit at me so I turned us over so I could take the lead again.

"You want me to fuck you into oblivion Mouth, is that it?" Her answer was to put her legs up over my shoulders grab my ass and pull me tighter against her.

"Oh fuck." Whether I wanted to or not, it was on. I pounded her like my dick had something to prove, she stayed with me all the way, her pussy was working the fuck outta me. If this was a fight I'm not sure who the winner was, we fucked each other till we were both cumming and growling and screaming. I was the growler that time.

We spent all day in bed, her appetite was out of control and my dick was all kinds of happy, the bed was a wreck, my back was protesting but I paid that shit no mind and my cock realized that although he was sore, if we fucked in water it was all good.

"Flanagan, I think you've achieved your goal already, I can't get pregnant twice, you keep that thing away from me. You have to carry me back to bed because I can barely move."

"No problem baby momma." I don't know how the fuck I was supposed to do that when I had no strength left myself, but I'll try.

Sleep came easily that night after a light snack, neither of us wanted too much to eat although we'd expended all our energies throughout the day and well into the night.

I slept like a baby and didn't know shit until about seven the next morning. I smacked Mouth on the ass as I climbed out of bed, she grumbled at me and rolled over, burying her head under her pillow; I guess I was making breakfast this morning.

I was just turning pancakes over onto a warmer when she came into the kitchen and my phone rang simultaneously.

I had on sweats and a tee while she was still in her robe.

"Hi baby, let me get this and I'll get you some juice, sit down."

She looked a little strange but did as I said, I wonder what that was about, couldn't be morning sickness, I think it was too early for that, whatever.

"Flanagan." Michael was on the other end.

"James is dead."

"Who, what the fuck, my little brother?" I heard a strange noise behind me but paid it no mind.

"No, Foster."

"What, how?" Fuck I wanted to do that fucker myself.

"Bow and Arrow." I listened as he gave me the details of the killing while I turned and looked at Mouth trying to piece shit together. It couldn't be, there's no way, how, when?

"How long was he there?"

"It's a new hit, hours maybe."

We both knew who had done it, what I didn't understand was how. I hung up the phone as I looked at her fully.

"How'd you do it Arianna?"

She turned innocent eyes up to me and that's when I knew for sure, innocent my ass.

"Do what?"

"Do not fuck with me Arianna."

"I don't know what..."

"Don't fucking lie to me, don't you do it, you didn't kill James last night or early this morning?" She kept quiet and that was all the answer I needed.

I left the room and headed for the bedroom, fuck this shit, I needed to get out and clear my fucking head because I didn't know what the fuck I was dealing with here.

I took down an overnight bag and put my shoes on before heading for the front door.

"Shane where are you going?" She grabbed the tail of my shirt.

"Away from you, you fucking disappoint me." I shook my head at her and ignored the look of hurt that came across her face.

"Shane please..."

"No, you drop me a line in a few months and let me know if my kid survived your bullshit so I can arrange for child support or some shit, bye."

I pulled the door open and headed out, Mouth right behind me and walked right into danger. I had my piece in hand and was firing before the fingerless fuck was able to get one off.

I felt her body shaking behind me, for someone who killed so effortlessly she sure had a strange reaction to violence.

"Ssh, come here, it's okay, we're okay." I pulled her body into my chest and tried to sooth her; this shit couldn't be good in her condition.

Without sparing another look for the dead goon in my hallway I walked her backwards into the apartment.

"Breathe baby."

"He was, I wasn't, what if?" She shook like a leaf as she rambled; I knew what she was trying to say. We were almost ambushed, she hadn't been prepared.

Right now my only concern was the safety of her and our child, I knew enough to know that this type of stress wasn't good for them.

"Babe, you gotta breathe, look at me, breathe in, hold it, breathe out, keep looking at me, there's nothing else, just you me and him." I put my hand over her flat tummy.

"You with me, it's all about him, you get overexcited he doesn't stand a chance against that kind of stress, knock it back babe."

I pulled out my phone while I held her against me.

"I need clean up at my place." I closed the phone and headed to the couch with her in my arms. We sat like that until she calmed down and I could think once more.

"I'm done."

"Thank fuck." I knew what she meant; she was done with her vigilante bullshit.

"Are you still gonna leave me?"

"The bag's empty Mouth."

"The...you..." She tried taking a swing at me.

"Settle your ass down, the guys will be here any minute to take that piece of shit outta here, when they're done I'm packing your ass up and moving you to the estate, maybe being surrounded by peace and serenity will do something for your murderous tendencies." She had the nerve to snort.

"Or you could take up hunting since you're so blood thirsty, my poor kid is fucked and he isn't even here yet."

"Hey, what do you mean by that?"

"Where's your bow babe, you not planning to pin my ass to the wall by way of my neck are you? What I mean is that instead of a mom who bakes him cookies and sings him lullabies, he'll have you, at least my mom and sisters will be there to give the little tyke all the motherly love he needs." Who said I had to fight clean? This chick is certifiable, I've been saying it since the day we met, now I know how true that shit is, she's beyond anything I've ever seen or heard of. I can't use the usual tactics on her because they don't work, it's like an on going battle, obviously I'm paying for some past sin or some shit.

"I can be motherly."

"Yeah, was it a mother who went out and nailed James to the wall in an alley, how the fuck did you find him there anyway?"

"You sure you want to know?"

I just gave he my don't fuck with me look.

"Okay, okay geez, I lured him there."

"How?"

"I pretended to be Teresa with new information on me, hah he took the bait, you should've seen his face when I showed up, I was on top of one of the buildings, I called down to him and when he turned I let him have it. No muss, no fuss."

"Baby, you do know you're a little touched right?"

"I'm not crazy Flanagan, I just like to get shit done, same as you, you just don't like it because I'm a girl."

"No, because you're my girl."

"Maybe we can work something out..."

"Hell no, you just told me you were done,...I give up, obviously this thing is bigger than I, you don't care what I think so it's up to you, like I said, my mom will take care of junior and make sure he gets all the TLC he needs while you do your thing."

"No one's raising my kid but me, I said I was done didn't I?"

"I think I heard that before, you're not too big on keeping your word."

"Are you calling me a welsher, if I say I'm done then I'm done."

"Like I said, heard that lie before, not falling for it again, just please try to give my kid a chance at life before you get him killed."

She looked at me like I'd slapped her, honestly, I didn't give a fuck, this girl wasn't like me or anyone I knew, she'd fucked me into a coma and went out and killed a mother fucker, all in a days work.

"That's just plain mean, try to get this through your head, James was a threat, do you think he would've let what you did to him in the club go? He would've always been plotting against you..."

"Wait a minute, you killed him because of me?"

"Well duh."

"Mouth, I'm not your father, you don't have to kill to protect me, I've been protecting me for a long mother fucking time, it's my job to protect you, and now this little one, what is it with you, why can't you get it?"

"I'm trying, besides you just killed fingers."

"Yeah mouth, that's what I do, what I'm trying to stop doing, getting out of the life so we can have one. I don't think you kill for the reasons you gave me, I think you're just a killer, plain and simple, like it's in your DNA, fuck...she's gonna train my kid to do this shit." Yes I'm laying it on strong; it's the only way to get through to mouth.

"I will not, you really think so?"

"I don't think you can help it, poor kid. It's kinda sad really, I had all these hopes and dreams for our off spring."

"Yeah, like what?"

"Oh I don't know, like maybe our sons and daughters could run the legitimate businesses that I've been grooming, not just the club but the restaurants and the art gallery, stuff like that, whatever they wanted to do, as long as it was legit. They'd play soccer and be in the school plays and maybe we'd get a little ballerina out of the bunch. We'd give them the best childhood ever, full of love while spoiling them rotten."

"I'd like that, I didn't have that, that sounds good, well dad and uncle Al and my aunt tried to spoil me, but there was too much of the other for it to be a really great childhood."

"Well, I guess we can always watch Sophie and Anna's kids have that kind of childhood...."

"What, why?"

"Well, if we're going to carry on with this mob shit..."

"No, no we're not either. I want our little ballerina."

Gotcha.

Chapter 13

The Assassin

Mob boy has lost his damn mind, he actually ordered these guys to come and pack us up.

No sooner had the dead goon's carcass been dragged away than these beef necked hoods, (I know a hood when I see one) were at the door with boxes and scowls that would scare small children.

"Mrs. Flanagan...."

"Come on in guys." He answered from behind me before I could correct the man's assumption that I was the little wife.

I heard a whispered 'is that her' before the three men turned and looked at me before being hustled off by the Don.

"What have you been telling these people about me?"

"Uh Mouth, we're not known for bow and arrows around these parts, two in quick succession and obviously by the same hand will bring speculation and being in our line of business, we have to keep up on the latest news if you know what I mean, so if you didn't want people knowing you as the Archer, you should've kept your ass in the house."

"Aren't you afraid I'll pin you to the wall next, seeing as how you're always in my face?"

"Mouth, you just iced a guy because you 'thought' he was a threat to me, I think I'm pretty safe."

I squinted my eyes at him, "I'm not sure about this relationship shit, if the other person knows you so well they might start to take advantage." I started mumbling under my breath, I was gonna have to figure this crap out, no way was I gonna let mob boy get the drop on me.

"Come here mouth, I read up on this shit and you're not supposed to become hormonal for at least another few months, so please, your special brand of crazy is enough to deal with don't add anything else just yet, let's get moved in and settled. ..."

"I don't see why we have to move it doesn't make sense."

"Because I say so, that's why."

Prince of The City

I should've known better yes, but where's the fun in that? I fielded the little paperweight that came at my head just as the sisters in law were coming through the door.

Michael the ass started grinning while Anthony tried to keep a straight face.

"Hey Archer, trying out for a new sport, the shot puck maybe?" Oh he thought that was funny, jackass.

"You two do what I asked?"

"Yep, all squared away."

"What did you tell them to do?"

"None of your concern babe, just go make sure the men are taking everything, they have to go to your apartment next and pick up your crap."

"I don't really have much over there, most of my things are back home in Chicago, maybe I can..."

"Stuff it killer, you're not going anywhere, I'll hire professionals to pack up your shit when the smoke clears and your father goes back home."

"Fine." She huffed her way into the bedroom grumbling all the way.

"Where're the twins?"

"Bringing up the rear, they're still pissed that she got past them to do Foster, they're trying to figure it out."

"Get them in here, they'll never figure that shit out and trying to figure her out could take a lifetime, shit I was asleep next to her and didn't hear a thing."

"I heard that mob boy, just you wait."

"Oh shit Shane, you better watch it, I don't fancy having to unpin your ass from a wall, that shit is ghastly, speaking of which, here." Anthony threw an envelope at me.

Inside were pictures of James, pinned to a wall by his fucking neck, eyes and mouth opened as if in surprise. She'd nailed him dead center of his throat.

"What's in those fucking things that they can hold a grown man up like that?"

"That's just it, I think that shit is heavier than she is, I don't know how she does it, but I heard the guys talking and it takes some serious skill to do this shit."

"I can teach you Mikey." She sauntered back into the room with a backpack over her shoulder.

"You're not teaching anyone anything, we're going to swing by the craft store and get you some yarn so you can learn to make booties, what's in the bag?" The two fucks started laughing.

"Stuff...."

"Quit fucking around Mouth, what you got, I don't recall ever seeing that bag before." I pulled it off her shoulder and out of her reach.

"Holy shit Arianna, what the fuck?" I turned the bag so Michael and Anthony could see the contents just as Zane and Alec came in. I'd left the door open since the place would be crawling with my men all day with this moving shit and we'd pretty much taken care of the enemy quota for at least another couple days.

"That's an assassin's cache boss."

"You think Alec?" I passed the bag off to him and turned to the terror that was mine.

"You give that back."

"What do you need it for, huh?" I made a point of eyeing her stomach when I said it to drive the point home.

"Hey kids what's going on? Ari I hear you nailed another one."

Her father and uncle along with my Poppy came through the door; maybe I should rethink this open door shit.

"Hey dad, don't talk about it, it makes Leonidas over here nervous?"

"Leonidas?"

"Yeah you know, the Spartan king, fought with the three hundred against Xerxes of Persia."

"Kid where do you come up with this shit?"

"I'm a genius uncle Al, didn't you know?"

She grinned at the two men like we weren't just discussing her little bag of destruction.

"So you're moving to the estate, that's good, it'll be harder for the enemy to get to you there."

"Thanks for the update Poppy, anything new on your end?"

"Let's go talk in private, you don't mind do you Archer?" He laughed his old ass off at that, fucking archer.

"Man news travels fast, you three been gossiping again? Dad where've you been, what's going on back home? Stalin over here won't tell me anything."

"And he's not gonna tell you anything either, you're out of it, done." I turned and headed to my office followed by the three meddling fucks, who knows what they had up their sleeves this time, it was always something with them, between them and Mouth I don't know how I have time for anything else.

"Okay let's have it."

"What little Shane, it's nothing, we just wanted to have a little chat that's all."

"Okay so spill it."

"Well, we all agree that you're just the man to tame the Archer, but...."

"Wait Poppy, you knew about this shit?" He didn't have to answer; the guilty flush on his face said it all.

"Never mind, carry on." I held the bridge of my nose between my thumb and forefinger where I could feel a headache coming on.

"Well, as I was saying, we think just cutting her off cold turkey might not be the way to go, you see, you have to wean her off these things, little by little, it's like you, you can't just go legit, you have to maneuver things around and set things up just right before that can happen, just as with her...."

"Poppy what bullshit, it's only the business part of things that takes time, but I can keep myself from going out and offing a motherfucker if I choose to."

"Yeah, then why do you have guys in Chicago right now?"

"Because those fucks back there are a threat to my wife and besides if I don't do it, she will and I'd be damned if I let that happen."

"Son, you're forgetting one thing."

"And what's that Rossi?"

"She's not yours yet."

"Are you fucking kidding me, she's all mine, has been from the moment we met and last night we confirmed that she's with child so tell me again how she's not my wife."

"You hear that Al, we'll soon have another one, a little Ari running around, maybe we can..."

"No, you can't, whatever it is you're thinking you can forget it, you're not turning my kid into a fucking killing machine."

"Son you sound like you resent her for..."

"Not her, you, I resent the fuck out of you two for putting her in this position, for making her believe that this was the only way, now I have to clean up your fucking mess, a fucking nineteen year old girl just iced three people in less than a week, that I know of, as for your bullshit poppy, you can't tame a lion after he's tasted human blood, you have to cut the motherfucker's head off one time..."

"What the fuck Flanagan you talking about killing my kid?"

"No you ass, I'm saying you have to cut her off one time, there's no weaning her, we're not talking about breaking someone of a bad habit, we're talking about a fucking killing machine that needs to be stopped. What's she gonna do, strap my kid onto her back and go out hunting? You two have no idea of what you spawned do you? Do you even understand what she is? She's stone cold, even I have a give a fuck meter, I think things through, weigh the options, try to find redeeming qualities at least before I off someone, not Mouth. She perceives a threat, she eliminates can you imagine some other kid fucking with ours? Let's say the kids are into sports and some kid tackles Shane junior on the field, Mouth would straight up off him and probably do the parents too."

"Don't you think that's a bit of an exaggeration?"

"Fuck you Alphonso, you know damn well it isn't, she's locked into her fucking head, all kidding aside, I play it easy with her, but I can see what not even she sees, she's locked into her fucking head and I have to find the key. I have some ideas, but you three fucks stay out of it...."

"What do you mean locked into her head?"

"I mean that something happened in her childhood that set the precedent for all this, somehow she's gotten it into her head that killing is her only chance at survival, it's them or her, she perceives a threat, she removes that threat. Permanently. Now unless you know what the fuck that is, I'll thank you three to leave me to deal with my woman how I see fit."

"Boy you sure do have balls I'll give you that."

"Rossi, if you weren't her father I would've already capped your ass."

Why that should make the three yentas howl with laughter was beyond me, but then again I was surrounded by crazy ass people, I should get used to it. Speaking of which I better go see what the mouthy one was up to.

Chapter 14

"Mouth what the fuck are you watching, oh hell no, turn that shit off you do not need any ideas."

"Touch it and die Luciano, you feeling lucky?"

Fuck now she's dirty Harry; I ignored her ass and turned the TV off, she did not need to be watching the Godfather, I think she was spoon fed that shit as a toddler.

We've been moved in for two weeks, the situation in Chi town had been taken care of, the three old fucks had been there and back since then, now Mouth and I were supposed to go look over the operation there, Rossi had supposedly cleaned up his shit and I was getting my shit done, mouth hadn't offed anyone in a while that I know of, but I had my guys on her ass like white on rice, these days she went no farther than my mom's next door or to one of the girls.' She seemed to be doing just fine at the compound for all the griping she'd done in the beginning, pain in the ass.

"I'm hungry feed me."

Yeah that's another thing, she's milking this pregnancy shit for all it's worth, what a racket, all hours of the day it's feed me thus and get me that; not that I mind though, I get a kick out of it, I also love fucking her knowing my kid is in there plus she's horny as fuck too.

"What do you want to eat mama?"

"Fried chicken."

"You're not eating fried chicken for breakfast mouth, get the fuck outta here."

She threw a pillow at my head and turned her movie back on. "Pie will make me some if I ask."

That's true, my mom's new kick is spoiling the fuck out of my girl, in fact it seemed like since news of the baby got out and about everyone was trying to spoil her little ass.

"Fruit you're having fruit and some oatmeal."

"I'm not eating no stinking oatmeal Cochise, now get me the colonel."

"Arianna, cut the shit, who the fuck is at the door now?"

"Probably dad and uncle Al."

"The fuck they want?"

"Be nice."

The two old reprobates came through the door.

"Where's the other one?" I'd grown accustomed to seeing Poppy with them everywhere now.

"Talking to your dad, we need to talk Flanagan."

"Not here." I looked at Mouth, she wasn't allowed around any business talk, she got too many fucking ideas so it was best not to tempt her.

"Read your bride magazine babe."

The wedding was in the works, mom and the girls were all over it, Mouth was playing neutral but that was okay, I understood that it was her way of safe guarding herself, she'd show up and say her I do but until the deed was done my little scared girl was going to pretend indifference.

"Ok what's the problem now?" We'd made it to my office with the doors closed.

"You have a congressman that's not too happy with the new order of things, he's making waves, your Poppy thinks we can work things out, I think the guy just wants more money, but it's been my experience that these fucking snakes never stop, they just keep coming back."

"So what're you saying Rossi?"

"I'm saying I've taken care of my end of things you and Ari just have to take the helm, there will be no backlash I made sure of it, everything is legit right across the board on my end, my little grand baby will be inheriting a legit operation, we've taken care of everything here along with your Poppy, all but this one guy."

"Don't even think about mentioning this shit to Mouth, she'd have his ass pinned to a wall somewhere before I can even blink."

They exchanged a look between them.

"Don't even think about it you fucks, I'll have your asses."

"We didn't sat anything."

"Mouth get the hell away from that damn door." I just knew she was listening in to this conversation.

"Who says I'm listening mob boy?" I just rolled my eyes at her bullshit.

"If I see on the news a congressman's been offed I'll tan your ass, no joke."

She stomped back into the other room fussing.

"And cut that shit out, no stomping until after the baby comes.

Chapter 15

"Fuck, shit, fuck, fuck."

"Mouth what the fuck? She'd scared me awake with her screaming, there were torn books and magazines all over the place and her pillow was a feathery mess on the floor.

"What's gong on?"

"I can't do this shit, it's driving me fucking crazy."

"What's driving you crazy babe?"

"All this wedding shit, I'm buried under tulle and organza and what the fuck...."

"Buried, who's buried, who'd you ice now Mouth?" Why that should cause crazy lady to try to brain me with a lamp is anybody's guess but that's what I get for sleeping with a nut job.

"Nobody's been buried you ass, it's material, it's what they make wedding dresses out of. I can't, I just....arrgggghhhhhhh....." I was off the bed and pulling her into me before she could pull her hair out at the roots.

"Stop baby, what's going on?" I tried talking over her screams and pulling her hands out of her hair.

"Mommy, I want my mommy."

"What the fuck!" I took us both down to the floor when she started shaking hard; I didn't know what was going on here but I knew it wasn't good. My first instinct was to get my father here quick so I scooted over to the nigh stand with her clutched in my arms and got my phone.

"Dad something's going on with Mouth...she just started screaming and pulling her fucking hair now she's screaming for her mom but I'm pretty sure her mom's dead."

"I'll be right there son just keep holding her." I hung up the phone and wrapped both arms around her.

"It's okay baby, help's on the way."

My spitfire girl curled into me and scared the fuck outta me.

"Mama, mama." She kept up a moaning chant for her mother that broke my fucking heart; by the time dad arrived I was ready to throw myself off the fucking roof.

"Let me have a look son."

I got up with her in my arms and laid her on the bed, dad checked her over while I watched.

"I think she's in some kind of shock, what happened?"

"I don't know we were asleep and she woke me up with her screams, the room was a mess and she was talking about the wedding and screaming for her mother." Now I was the one pulling on my hair.

"Let her rest son, I'm going to give her something mild, we have to think about the baby. Maybe with everything happening so fast and all at once she's had some sort of break." Dad fussed around her for a bit more before leaving me alone with her; I stood there and watched her chest rise and fall with every breath my mind in a daze. What the fuck just happened? Obviously it has something to do with her mother who come to think of it I don't really know all that much about, all I know is that she's gone as in dead but that's about it; somehow I always just assumed that she'd been sick, why I never dug deeper I don't know I just never thought of it. It could be because Arianna never made an issue of it, that was obviously a huge mistake on my part something I was gonna have to get to the bottom of.

I was tempted to call her father and uncle but squashed the impulse, I needed to be with her right now and I didn't need her overhearing what I might have to say to those two fucks. I laid down next to her and eased her into my arms, she drew in one long deep breath her lips moved into a Cupid bow pout and she settled down again. My sweet baby, what the fuck had set her off?

I needed to throw a punch but at what? There wasn't any physical threat, according to dad something might've broke in her head how do I fight that shit? I'm not going to get too worried about it, whatever it is I'm sure we can beat it together I won't settle for anything less; besides she's too fucking strong to lose her mind.

I can't even think about that shit right now, we have a baby coming, a wedding to plan, the future to look forward to no way was I losing her to whatever the fuck is in her head.

I don't know how long we laid there with me tracking her heartbeats, watching her face for any sign that she was in distress, but so far she seemed okay, whatever dad had given her had calmed her down. I was a little worried for my kid but there wasn't much I could do at this point other than look after both of them.

"Shane?"

"Yeah baby I'm right here how're you feeling?" I pulled her up higher on my chest so I could see into her eyes; still a little clouded over but my baby was in there.

"What happened?" She looked around at the room confused.

"Uh babe, do you remember anything from this morning?" She looked a little lost there for a minute before rubbing her temple as if in pain.

"I have a terrible headache but that's about it was I sick? I feel like I was sick."

Shit, dad didn't leave any instructions on how to handle these kinds of questions, I mean am I supposed to tell her that she'd had a psychotic break or some shit or play it off like it was nothing major? I'm not too comfortable with the idea of lying to her so I went with the truth.

"You had a slight episode baby."

"Episode, what episode, what are you talking about?"

"Well I woke up to you screaming for your mom and tearing the room apart."

"What, my mom, what about my......?" She clutched her head as it fell to my chest; Fuck this shit, her body started trembling hard as fuck so I wrapped us both up in the covers and held on tight, scared out of my fucking mind again. When she started moaning and rocking back and forth on my chest I felt tears in my eyes.

"No, no, no, no, no, come on baby come back." I kept repeating that over and over again.

"I love you Mouth you hear me, I love you more than anything in this world, do you know before I met you I never thought there was a woman out there for me, never thought I'd find my perfect match but you're it, my perfect mate; you're the best thing to ever happen to me do you know that? As long as I live I'll never stop being grateful for your coming into my life and no matter what this is we'll get through it and we'll be stronger and better."

I sent up a quick prayer that this would be true. She quieted down some at the sound of my voice now she just hiccupped in her sleep as she'd fallen off again. I eased my hand out from the cocoon I'd made with the covers and reached for my phone on the nightstand again, speaking as softly as possible so as not to wake her but still enforce steel into my voice I gave my command.

"Come to the compound now and bring your sidekick with you."

"Shane.... what?"

"Now!" I cut her father off and hung up.

"It's okay baby we'll figure it out." I brushed the hair back off her face and closed my eyes for a moment of peace.

Chapter 16

Prince of The City

Hoping that she'd stay asleep long enough for me to do what needed to be done I went to answer the door. I didn't even want to leave her for the few minutes it took to do that but at least I had the monitor with me.

My first sight of the two reprobates had me seeing red; my first inclination was to wrap my hands around their fucking throats and squeeze but I wouldn't get any answers that way so I reeled it in.

"Flanagan, what the fuck?"

"What happened to her mother?" No preambles; I didn't have time for that shit, I wanted answers, needed them in fact and now. I saw the faltered steps in both men; the little sideways look that was fleeting but not quick enough for me to miss.

They brushed pass me to get inside still not uttering a word; that's not how this was going to go down; I've been pretty lenient with these fuckers up 'til now but I had no problem showing them why I was who I am for so long, family or not, when it comes to her all fucking bets are off; and that bullshit I witnessed this morning had to be dealt with. I needed to get to the bottom of this shit so I could help my girl deal with whatever the fuck was up. These fucks lied to me, when I told them there was something in her head they fucking played it down they had to have known that whatever this was, it was bad.

"Start talking motherfuckers and no beating around the bush and before you start this is not Shane you're talking to, this is Flanagan, know the fucking difference."

"Alright calm down young'un."

"Don't fucking tell me to calm the fuck down...just tell me what I want to know, what happened to her mother and no bullshit."

"You have to give us a minute here son, this isn't easy for us either you know."

"You're a grown fucking man Rossi, right now I don't give a shit about you, I do care about the nineteen year old girl that had a fucking breakdown of monumental proportions not too long ago, now you two think you can get your heads out of your asses long enough to tell me what the fuck is going on here?"

"Shit, we knew this day might come Roberto, it was only a matter of time..."

"Hey Alphonso; don't talk to him, talk to me, what the fuck happened to her?"

"We'll tell you son, but I'm gonna need a drink for this." He went to the sidebar and poured a stiff scotch while Rossi found a seat and sat with his head in his hands. All these theatrics just made me nervous as fuck I mean what could make two die-hard mobsters this shaken? Rossi looked like he was barely gonna make it and Alphonso wasn't faring much better.

I watched them with bated breath knowing that whatever was coming next was going to be some horrible shit and that somehow at the end of it, I was going to have to pick up the pieces for my girl; I didn't mind that so much I just wanted to know what the fuck so I could get started fixing shit.

"Arianna saw her mother die."

Well fuck me; Rossi divulged that information in the voice of a man who'd aged fifty years since he came through my door ten minutes ago. I hardened myself enough to withstand what was coming next; I didn't utter a word just waited for one or the other to pick up the story because I knew there had to be more.

"She was only three, at first we thought she'd forgotten that night, but as time went on she started acting strange though she'd never mention it, just little things that told us it was affecting her ya know?"

"Like what?"

"You know, she'd act out, have these horrible tantrums, sometimes she'd scream and scream and when we asked her what the problem was she'd say nothing or she didn't remember. We messed around with taking her to a shrink for a while but in the end it was too risky. Back then there were things going on that we couldn't afford to let out of our circle, who knew what she would share with a stranger and what he might do with it? We couldn't trust our own guys at the time and there was no way we could risk an unknown, you know the deal, it was a fucked up time."

I wanted to be mad at him but the reality was in our line of business there were sometimes hard choices that had to me made, it was for shit, but I understood.

"What did she see?"

Rossi put up his hand as if to ward me off, his other hand went to his stomach as if in pain. If he was having a hard time telling the rest of the story I could only imagine what she'd been living with in her head all these years.

"It's okay Roberto I'll tell him the rest."

"She saw her mother lose her head."

Alphonso said it quickly like he had to get the taste out of his mouth, the words slammed into my body like blows from a two by four. Now it all made sense, a lot of things fell into place for me with that one sentence.

"Did you get them?"

They knew what I meant by that, I think I already knew the answer though and if I was right I was gonna have to change my stance on some things; looked like I wasn't quite through being me yet, fuck.

"The one who called the hit yeah; but not the one who carried it out, we got most of the men who were there that night, but the one they named for the actual beheading we were never able to find him; he flew the coop, like the fucking wind, trust me we never stopped looking but we thought after all this time she'd forgotten."

"She hasn't forgotten shit, she's been eliminating him her whole fucking life, do you not notice a pattern in her kills; she always goes for the head."

Fuck me, I have a pregnant vigilante on my hands, she's not gonna stop, not because she doesn't want to, or because she wants to disobey me, but because it's damn near impossible for her to stop, until I find this fucker and take his ass out she's always going to be avenging her mother one way or the other.

I left them both sitting there with their memories and went to check on her; she was sound asleep, curled up around my pillow. Toeing off my shoes I climbed in behind her and drew her tight against me. Feeling the warmth of her body I inhaled her amazing scent.

"I'll find him for you mouth, I'll get you his fucking head."

I'm not sure if she heard me or not, but I'd be damned if her body didn't relax against mine.

Chapter 17

Whether she heard me in her sleep or not was still left to be seen but she was sure acting differently. She'd awakened from her drug-induced slumber like nothing happened. I kept watching and waiting for some sort of relapse but she was like a woman with a plan. Suddenly she was into wedding plans and babies; she was like a whirlwind all of a sudden with enough energy to keep me hopping. It was so astounding that I put her guards on high alert because who knows what the fuck she could get up to.

I had to leave her for a little while to go see about business but I didn't plan to be gone long; I'd used my phone and my extensive network of contacts to do some digging into her shit, first things first. I'd decided to put my shit on ice for the next little while, this shit that was fucking with her head was way more important than some congressman that was holding out for more.

Her father and uncle had given me all the latest info they had on the guy who'd done her mother but from what they told me he seemed to always be one step ahead of them, maybe that's because he knew to look for them, because he had to know that the mark they had on his head was for life, there was no pardon. I got a general description and a name and that was all I needed; I'll do the rest myself.

"Mouth what the fuck?"

"What?"

"What's all this?"

I'd left her alone; well not alone Alec and Zane were in the house somewhere, but I'd gone out to see about some shit that needed taking care of today, Intel had come in that might've been helpful. That was a surprise since apparently Rossi had been after this guy all these years and hadn't heard a peep and yet I was getting hits right off the bat. I couldn't have been gone more than two hours since I'd made it a point not to be gone from her for too long but I came back to a kitchen full of pies and other shit. I didn't even know she could do this shit.

I was looking at her a little warily I'm sure, I mean other men might be excited by this shit, me I was scared like a motherfucker, either that shit dad gave her was jacked or something had twisted in her head.

"It's cakes and pies and cookies." Just then the guys came into the kitchen, I could tell they'd been eating whatever the fuck she'd been baking because they had empty dishes and big ass grins on their faces. I checked them over to make sure my little spitfire hadn't pulled a fast one and slipped them something because sure as shit something was going on here or I'd woken up in the fucking twilight zone.

"You back to making me crazy again aren't you?"

"Boss, the Mouth can cook, just saying." Alec was still chewing.

They were looking over the rest of the shit she had spread out all over the counters and the island in the kitchen. How the fuck long was I gone anyway.

"What smells so good in here; damn Tony look at this shit."

My two sisters in law came in behind me and joined the other two at the trough, was I the only one that saw something wrong with this picture? They were all acting like this shit was normal. I snagged her around the waist and took her out of the room; cornering her against the wall in the hallway I had to first steal a kiss before interrogating her. She had flour on her nose, this shit was beyond scary.

"What are you up to baby girl?"

I couldn't go hard, I had to remember that just a few short hours ago she'd been sick, I wasn't too sure exactly where she was in her head, she hadn't even mentioned anything about her episode its almost as if she didn't remember or she just put it out of her head; I'm not sure which I preferred.

"Nothing, I'm in the mood to bake, I haven't done it since I moved here." She climbed to her toes and kissed me; what was I to do? I kissed her back, her explanation sounded good to me and if that shit made her happy then so be it.

My phone buzzed on my hip and I pulled it off while still sucking her face, my girl was in a mood, I might have to get rid of the guys.

I pulled away long enough to answer the phone but she started in on my ears.

"Flanagan."

"You offed the congressman? I thought we were going to handle it?"

"Poppy?"

I just looked at her, the sneak, I don't know how she fucking did it but I knew she did.

"Yeah, thing is this isn't your usual but we'll deal, not to worry tell the boys we've got clean up since they seem to have their heads up their ass, how many times I told you never leave anything behind?"

"Sorry about that poppy it won't happen again." I kept my eyes on hers; she was looking at me just a little warily now, biting into that lip of hers. I hung up the phone and just looked at her.

"What am I gonna do with you huh?"

"What?" She gave me the big wide eyes like she was innocent and shit.

"How'd you get out without them knowing?"

She didn't answer me so I used my arms that were wrapped around her to shake her a little.

"Answer me baby, how'd you do it, I'm not mad at you I just wanna know."

"Nope, if I tell you you'd know my secrets and what if I have to do it again?"

"Mouth I'll kick your ass, I'm not fucking around."

"The wedding's in a few weeks we don't need to have any loose strings, we're supposed to be starting over fresh for the baby which means we have to get all this shit done in a short time."

"How did you do it?"

"Seriously it doesn't take that long to kill somebody it's not like I went there to have a conversation with him or anything Charlie Luciano." I rolled my eyes at that, was she implying that that's what I did?

"How'd you know where to find him?"

"Google earth."

"Goo...fuck me sideways who else is on your hit list this week Aileen Wuornos?"

"Stop being so dramatic, he had to be dealt with and now it's done, one less thing for you to have to deal with, now I have to get my key lime pie out the oven before it burns."

I'm gonna fucking wring her damn neck, she's too fucking much, what the fuck?

I left her and went to the kitchen.

"I thought I told you fucks not to let her out of your sight?" They were both stuffing their faces again while Mikey and Tony were digging into what looked like chocolate pie.

"We didn't, she was in here the whole time." Zane looked back and forth between us puzzled.

"Well except for when she took her bath and asked us to watch the pies that they don't burn and put the others in." Alec piped in, poor sod; I could see how they would fall for that; they couldn't very well follow her in there unless they wanted me to plug their asses and she knows that too the sneak.

"Am I paying you to be a fucking cook?"

"Don't take it out on them it's not their fault."

"Yeah, well you just cost them their jobs."

"Wha...you can't, Shane don't do that." She looked back and forth between me and them; uh huh, I've got you now, found your weak spot.

I left the kitchen like I was really mad, I'd given the guys the look to let them know I was playing her, I couldn't very well fault them for this, she gets the drop on me too; it seems there's no way to contain the murderous little deviant.

She followed me out of the kitchen pleading with me not to fire the boys, I could tell that this was going to be my life, I could tell her to quit this shit a million times I could threaten I could lock her ass up somewhere, she'd still find a way. There was only one thing to do.

"Get packed, we're going to Chicago."

She stopped short; "You're kicking me out, you can't kick me out...."

I rolled my eyes again, since when had I picked up her annoying habit?

"I said we Mouth, now get your shit together; I know where Tommy the knife is." I said it fast in hopes that the blow wouldn't be too harsh but she still stumbled at the name. I looked back and took her hand pulling her along behind me.

"That's where I was this morning when I left you, I don't know how you missed him he's been in Wisconsin of all places all this time, not too close and not too far; he's still working for the mob...."

"You sure it's him?"

"I'm sure baby."

"But you were only gone for a few hours how could you find out so quickly?" She was crying again so I pulled her in and kissed her.

"Trust me, I know how important this is to you, I wouldn't fuck up, it's him. Now we can do this now or we can wait until after the wedding, your choice."

"Let's do it now so we can start fresh after the wedding, I want it all done and buried so we can move on; but, what the hell are we gonna do with ourselves now?"

"We'll figure it out, there has to be more to life than killing and shit."

"This going legit shit is the pits."

Who knew it would be harder for her than I?

THE END

You may contact the Author @

Jordansilver144@gmail.com

On her Facebook page@

https://www.facebook.com/MrsJordan Silver

Twitter handle is@JordanSilver144

If you enjoyed this story you might also like these titles by the Author

Lyon's Crew

Lyon's Angel

Lyon's Way

My Best Friend's Daughter

Loving My Best Friend's Daughter

Passion

Night Visits

The Claiming

And much more

Excerpt from Book 4 of The Spitfire Series The Family

Chicago isn't just windy, it's...something; there's an underlying tone of something very off about this place. Maybe it's the mobster in me or maybe it's because I know the history of the place so well, but I felt stifled here, couldn't wait to get the fuck out.

"We're in and out, I have everything in place for us so it should be a clean run."

"Flanagan you've said the same thing like fifteen times since we got on the jet, I'm about ready to stuff a sock in your craw."

She's a little nasty this morning, she had her first bout of morning sickness and what a delight that was. Somehow when a strong woman became ill it had more of an impact, of course it could also have to do with the fact that I tried to leave her ass behind after she'd been so sick. You'd think I'd slapped the shit out of her the way she reacted.

"Hey yenta one and two you two think you could maybe keep up here, this is not a sightseeing expedition."

"Sure bro, the girls gave us a list."

"What the fuck Anthony, a list of what?"

These fucks were trying to make me crazy, first I had to bring them because heaven forbid I should go anywhere on the map without their presence, then I had to bring the twins because they were Mouth's shadow from now on heaven help them. I've never heard so much muttering and complaining from two grown men in my life.

The six of us had taken my Lear jet to Chi town early this morning; we'd be holed up at a secret location chosen by her old man, not their mansion of course, we didn't want the fuckers to know we were on their turf, not until it was too late anyway. Mouth was chomping at the bit to get shit done, there was no use cautioning her or telling her to take it easy; in one ear and out the other.

"We're not fucking shopping you ass, are you kidding me what the fuck?" Okay I'm still a little raw after watching my girl be sick, I had no idea morning sickness was like that. She was damn near rolling around on the floor in pain. Of course I got the blame for that as soon as she was coherent again.

I could see why Alphonso had called my place a dump, if this was just a little get away spot then I'd hate to see where she'd lived before; not that my place was anything to sneeze at, but the Rossis were into some serious shit. The place was like something out of an old Roman flick or some shit, marble and gold, and her room was fucking huge.

"You spend a lotta time here Mouth?"

"When I was younger yeah, dad built it as sort of a getaway for me but I haven't been since I was like sixteen, why?"

I looked at her, fuck I'm gonna have to up my game, probably have to gut the house or some shit, or maybe level it and start from scratch.

"What're you thinking mob boy?"

"I might need to rebuild the house or some shit."

"You're an ass."

She just rolled her eyes and headed for the bathroom.

"Please don't do that throwing up thing again Mouth, I can't deal with that shit twice in one day."

She peaked around the door with a scowl.

"Are you bent, you can't deal with it? I'm the one up chucking you moron, this was your bright idea remember?"

Oh yeah that had been her argument this morning after her first bout of torture; my manhood had come into question among other things. I was just happy that whatever the fuck breakdown she'd had was out of the way though I still watched her to make sure she was okay. She was looking forward to ending the fucker that had ended her mother; somehow I didn't think shit would stop there, not with her murdering ass. I was afraid there was always gonna be someone else that got on her bad side and ended up on the wrong end of her bow and arrow.

I'd had a hell of a time getting her to leave that shit home but then she'd given in, a little too easily if you ask me but I'm not complaining.

I heard a lot of rummaging around and it sounded like she was tearing down the walls or some fuck.

"Mouth what the fuck?" I stepped into the bathroom in time to see her closing up a portion of the wall. There was a large black bag sitting at her feet, the shit looked heavy.

She bent to pick it up and I stopped her, taking it from her hand.

"Fuck Mouth what you got in here a body? And why the fuck you lifting this heavy shit? Ma said you're not supposed to remember?"

"It's not that heavy; tell me Don Luigi, you plan on being this annoying through this whole thing because if you are I'm moving in with Pia when we get back."

"Whatever."

By this time we'd reached the bed where I deposited the bag; she opened it and my mouth fell open.

"I thought you said you hadn't been here since you were sixteen?"

"Yeah so, and?"

"What the fuck Mouth, that's an arsenal in there, what sixteen year old girl stashes an arsenal?" Oh man I am so fucked, I'm gonna be cleaning up bodies for the rest of my life messing with this one.

"You do remember who my father is right? What, you thought I should leave my safety up to someone else? No way, I used to listen in on dad's conversations, I knew we could never really trust anyone except each other so I didn't trust anyone."

"What do you mean listen in on his conversations?"

"Sneak, once I wire tapped him but then I thought if the Feds ever got ahold of my stash he'd be gone forever so I stopped. What the hell's wrong with you mob boy?"

I had to sit down because my head had started pounding, fuck my life she's the female me.

"Mouth swear to me right here and now on our children that after this hit you're done."

"Thou shalt not swear."

CPSIA information can be obtained
at www.ICGtesting.com
Printed in the USA
FFOW03n0851150116
20490FF